THE FIRE CATCHER

ALGEBRA CARTER

To Evelyn, Hailey, Neha, and Nina, for being good friends.

And to my supportive sister, my best friend.

Best wishes,
algebra Carter

FOREWORD

Dear Reader,

I hope that as you read this book, you understand that a book takes a while to put together. Every day for 365 days, Algebra locked herself up in what was used to be called dad's office. But it is now called her office. And it took her many hours at a time to write this book. But when she went in her office, I found out she actually was writing more than one book at a time. I am surprised that she hasn't mixed up the plots yet!

With such intricate and intriguing plots, anybody would like her books. I remember seeing people reading *Liam Stone and Private Tower* who were seven years old, to people reading it at twelve, even adults. I just can't wait to see all of the people reading *The Firecatcher*. With characters such as Maddix, Luke, and Nicole, with their diverse personalities, this book is even harder to resist.

Maddix is such a strong character, even without

considering his special abilities. He is never stopped by his own fear, even when two scary guys are after him, trying to ruin his life. I think that is an amazing characteristic. I also think that Algebra Carter is like that. She never lets her fear get in the way of what she wants. She also never stops because something is just too much. I know this because every one of her books (that I have seen) have been finished (even though some of them end in a cliffhanger). Algebra definitely perseveres like that.

Algebra is the type of person to look up to. She has a creative mind and a great personality. Algebra is also very humorous and makes me laugh every minute I'm around her. All of those characteristics make her a great author. Her creative mind allows her to think of new and exciting stories that nobody has heard before. Her personality keeps the novel a book that everyone can relate to and is able to read. And her humor makes the book fun and enlightening for any age. I hope that you will see these characteristics as much as I do during this novel.

A book is a gift. It is a long and exciting adventure cut down to size. You are incredibly lucky to be on the verge of looking into a young boy's life and seeing how it feels to be in a world with interesting creatures, bad guys, and a touch of magic. You are in for a real treat!

-Algebra Carter's Sister
June 2017

Table of Contents

Foreword...*v*

Chapter 1 The Arising..*11*

Chapter 2 Zennith's Report..*18*

Chapter 3 The Explanation...*25*

Chapter 4 The Idea..*28*

Chapter 5 Disappointment...*33*

Chapter 6 The Antique Shop..*37*

Chapter 7 Griffin Calling...*45*

Chapter 8 Power Analyzation..*47*

Chapter 9 The Trouble with Teachers.................................*58*

Chapter 10 Confirmation...*68*

Chapter 11 F is for Foolish..*71*

Chapter 12 The Vision...*84*

Chapter 13 Thunderbirds...*88*

Chapter 14 Suspicions...*99*

Chapter 15 The Dark of The Night...................................*103*

Chapter 16 ~~Dagner~~ Danger...*109*

Chapter 17 Expectations..*118*

Chapter 18 Interrogation..*121*

Chapter 19 Criminal Minds..*124*

Chapter 20 Thoughts...*127*

Chapter 21 Interception..*131*

Chapter 22 To Talk or Not to Talk?..................................*133*

Chapter 23 Comeback..*140*

Chapter 24 The Return of The Thunderbirds......................*142*

Chapter 25 The Prophecy...*148*

Chapter 26 In Trouble...*151*

Chapter 27 Crystal Ball...*154*

Chapter 28 Expectant..*157*

Chapter 29 The View of an Outsider.................................*162*

Chapter 30 Lunges and Launches.....................................*165*

Chapter 31 The Ping-Pong Game 172

Chapter 32 The Wizard of Oz Method 175

Chapter 33 Sidelines 180

Chapter 34 The Firecatcher 182

Chapter 35 Kid in Black 188

Chapter 36 The Truth Hurts (So Much) 192

Chapter 37 Against ~~The Walls~~ Something More Dangerous Than Walls 196

Chapter 38 Ice and Burn 198

Chapter 39 Clockwise 201

Chapter 40 Throw-In 204

Chapter 41 Fireworks 218

Chapter 42 Inexplicable 221

Chapter 43 Caught 230

Chapter 44 In Trouble Again 232

Chapter 45 Flames and Whispers 235

Chapter 46 Anger and Fire 239

Chapter 47 Listen 242

Chapter 48 Disappointments 246

Chapter 49 Secrets Are Meant to Be Kept 249

Chapter 50 When You Never Listen 252

Chapter 51 Entry 257

Chapter 52 Sleepwalkers 260

Chapter 53 The Battle of the Enchanters 263

Chapter 54 The Room of Secrets 267

Chapter 55 Actors 273

Chapter 56 Mind Games 275

Chapter 57 In the Rubble 280

Chapter 58 The Secrets 282

Acknowledgements 288

About The Author 289

CHAPTER 1
THE ARISING

The swishing of a cloak. The feeling of purposefulness. The set face. The worries lost in the roaring wind. Sidero seemed to glide to the top of the mountain, where his human servant was to bring him news.

"Is everything going according to plan?"

"Yes, sire."

"And the boy?"

"Locked up, sire."

"Where?"

"In the old school. It hasn't been used in years."

"But will it reopen?"

"I doubt it."

"There is no room for doubt, Zennith. Are you completely sure it won't reopen?"

"I—yes, sire. I am completely sure."

"Good. Watch him and make sure he doesn't know anything."

"Of course, sire."

Sidero looked at his servant, as though daring him to ask why he must watch over the boy. But he didn't, so Sidero vanished. Zennith vanished as well. He reappeared in an abandoned tower of a large castle. Peeling letters above the large front doors read *Apollo Academy*. The school, as Zennith had said, hadn't been used in a long time.

Zennith looked at the boy. He had dark brown hair and round, hazel eyes. He also was looking around, like he wasn't in a dangerous place. Oh, but it was. Zennith remembered this boy's name. Sidero said that the boy's name was the least scary thing about him, but Zennith always felt chills go up his spine when he heard it (for reasons other than that the boy was his master's enemy). His name was Maddix Parker.

"Maddix! Hey, Maddix!" Lukas Vincent was slapping Maddix on the face. It had been years since Sidero told Zennith to keep a close eye on Maddix.

Since then, Apollo Academy had reopened. Maddix helped run it with his best friend, Luke Vincent, and Luke's father. Growing up in a school, he and Luke had long since mastered the coursework, and no longer attended class as students.

Maddix sat up and ran a hand through his dark hair. It stuck up at the back, along with many other places. Luke smiled. Today, Luke and Maddix were going to supervise a Mythology class taught by Mrs. Gilders. Maddix and Luke just sat at a small table and took notes.

"Settle down, class!" Mrs. Gilders exclaimed. Her class quieted and sat down in their seats. "Who studied for the test last night?"

Not many children raised their hands.

"Alright then," Mrs. Gilders said. "I guess you'll have to go with what you know, then." She placed a sheet of paper on each student's desk. Maddix wrote on his notepad, *One-sheet tests.* Luke wrote, *Students don't study.* The rest of the hour consisted of children's worried looks as they wrote things down on their sheet of paper, Maddix and Luke taking notes, and Mrs. Gilders reading a book entitled *Mythology Teaching Methods.* When the bell rang, Luke and Maddix took their notepads to Luke's dad. Mr. Vincent said, "Good work today, boys." But Maddix knew that he still didn't have the note-taking thing down. Soon, it was lunchtime, the only time that Luke and Maddix could talk about what was on each other's minds.

"So," Luke asked Maddix, "what's new?"

"Nothing much," Maddix said.

But as he said it, he remembered the dream he was having when Luke woke him up this morning.

He dreamt that a tall man was holding something—holding him!

And he saw a tower in his dream, a tower that looked like one of the many at Apollo Academy. But it *couldn't've* been at Apollo Academy. There were *tons* of towers around the world.

"Well, except that I had this really weird dream last night," Maddix told Luke. He explained the dream.

"That's weird! Do you know what it means?" Luke asked.

"No, what?" Maddix said.

"I don't know; I was asking you if you knew!"

Maddix thought. What *did* the dream mean? Was he going to be taken into a tower in the future? Or had it already happened? But how could he be sure the dream was real at all?

"Maybe we should ask my dad," Luke suggested.

"Okay," Maddix responded. They hurried to Mr. Vincent's office. On their way, they bumped into a girl with blonde hair in a braid.

"Watch where you're going!" she exclaimed.

"Sorry," Luke said. He turned to Maddix and muttered, "Students these days." When they reached Luke's father's office, they found Mr. Vincent himself sitting in a high-backed chair, typing on a computer.

"Hey, Dad," Luke said, to announce their presence. Mr. Vincent looked up.

"Hey, Luke," he said. "What's up? Is something wrong?"

"No," Luke shook his head. "Maddix and I were just wondering about something."

"What is it?" Mr. Vincent asked. Maddix told him about the dream. Afterward, Luke's father said, "Did it seem as realistic as it possibly could be, Maddix?" Maddix nodded. "Did it seem like it could happen?"

"Well, kind of. I mean, it was in a *tower...*"

"But, towers are real, aren't they?"

"Yeah, but it doesn't seem like it could really happen."

"If it seemed realistic, then it could occur, but we never know."

Maddix thought, *So the dream IS real. Towers are real, it's possible to be taken—even if it's unlikely—and I'm real, too.* But then, he remembered another thing from his dream: The tall man was holding a *baby*! It *couldn't've* been him! Yet, the baby *did* look identical to Maddix. Maddix told Mr. Vincent about the baby. "Very interesting," he said. "If the baby was indeed identical to you, there's no reason why we shouldn't believe it was you. Unless you have a twin?" Maddix shook his head.

"There you go," Mr. Vincent said. "Now, if you'll excuse me, I need to meet with someone. They have a girl your age—would you like to meet her?" Luke shrugged and Maddix said, "Sure."

Suddenly, there was a knock on the door.

"They're here!" Mr. Vincent exclaimed. He pulled open the door to reveal a blonde-haired woman, a brown-haired man, and *the same blonde-haired girl Luke and Maddix had bumped into!*

"Oh," Luke murmured, "she *isn't* a student." The girl looked at them, then remembered how they'd first met. Her eyes widened, and she pointed to them and shouted, "You!"

Maddix and Luke pointed to her and said, "You!" back.

"Have they met?" the woman asked Mr. Vincent.

"I don't know," Mr. Vincent replied. He turned to Maddix and Luke. "Have you?" The girl, Maddix, and Luke said, "Yes."

"This is Nicole," the man said.

"This is Luke, my son, and Maddix Parker," Mr. Vincent said.

"What's *she* doing here?" Luke asked rudely.

"*I* am here to help my dad inspect this school," she said. Maddix and Luke turned to Mr. Vincent.

"Inspect this school?" Luke repeated. "You never told me Apollo was to be inspected!"

"Boys, I know this may come as a surprise, but it's going to be okay—"

"So, we might lose this place?" Maddix asked.

"I—it'll be fine," Mr. Vincent reassured them. But Luke and Maddix weren't convinced. Nicole turned to the man (her father) and asked, "Dad, where do we start?" Then she looked at Luke and Maddix. She glared at them. They glared back. Nicole's father said to Mr. Vincent, "You said you had notes on teachers and classrooms?"

"Yes," Mr. Vincent replied. He turned to Luke and Maddix. "Show Mr. Rader your notepads, please."

"Rader," Luke muttered bitterly, "sounds right." Maddix nodded.

"Here you go, sir," Maddix and Luke handed their notepads to Mr. Rader.

"Thank you," he responded.

"Boys," Mr. Vincent said, "why don't you give Nicole a tour? I think it's better for the inspection." Mr. Rader nodded and said to his daughter, "Nicole, go with Maddix and Luke."

Maddix, Luke, and Nicole stomped out the door.

CHAPTER 2
ZENNITH'S REPORT

It had been ten years since Zennith had stolen Maddix Parker and taken him to the Apollo West tower. He thought that Sidero should know that Will Vincent might lose the school. Parker had nowhere else to go, so it was important to save Apollo Academy. Sure, he could stay at the Vincent's, but would Sidero and his followers be able to track him? Zennith called, "Sidero!" into the air, and the intimidating enchanter appeared.

"You called?"

"Sire—Apollo Academy—it might close!" Zennith exclaimed, getting down to business at once.

"How did you find out about this?"

"I saw inspectors! And I heard the conversation! Sire, if it closes, or gets run by someone else, we couldn't track the boy anymore—"

"Calm yourself, Zennith. We will fix it." Sidero said.

"But *how*, sire?" Zennith asked.

"We will simply place a tracking device on the boy." Sidero replied, like this was the easiest thing in the world.

"A tracking device? How?" Zennith wanted to know.

"You could place it on him." Sidero said.

"Will it stay? Will he suspect anything?"

"It will stay because it will be a special tracking device. He won't suspect anything."

Zennith was doubtful.

"How can you be so sure? I mean, you must have a *reason* to feel so sure of yourself."

"He won't suspect anything because he doesn't know we exist. And also, he won't notice it."

"Where will we put it, sire?" Zennith asked.

"Where do you think?"

Zennith thought for a moment. Then he said, "Oh! Okay. Where is it?"

Sidero pulled out a tracking device from one of his pockets and handed it to Zennith, who wondered what made it special. It probably had maximum stickiness or something.

"How will I get it on him, sire?"

"In the night, you will go into his bedroom by window, and place it on his ankle."

"Yes, sire." Zennith vanished. He reappeared at the top of Apollo Academy's North tower.

"What's the time?" he wondered aloud. He looked at his watch. It was twelve thirty in the afternoon. Zennith groaned. *It's going to be a LONG day.* He peered through the nearest window and found himself looking into a classroom. It was empty—except for three kids.

"Ha!" Zennith said under his breath. He had looked into the very window that showed him a classroom with Maddix, Luke, and Nicole in it.

"Seriously, Nicole," Luke was saying, "do you *really* want this school to close?"

Nicole chewed on her lip, contemplating her answer. "*Closed* isn't the right word," she said. "My dad just wants to take your dad's place, so he can run it."

"But why?" Maddix asked.

"Money," Nicole answered. "We'll get money because kids have to pay for textbooks and stuff."

"And you can't do anything to stop it?" Luke said.

"If I could, I wouldn't," Nicole responded, sounding genuinely honest. "Dad says that if I help inspect, I'll take your place with being top helper in running it. He says it'll be good for me to see how the school works here."

"Wait a second," Maddix said. "You're only inspecting this place, right? You're not saying it's even *gonna* be run by your dad today!"

Nicole looked at Maddix for a moment, chewing on her lip again. "Actually, we are," she said, almost sounding sorry for him. "My dad says that, no matter what, this school's going to run by him, even if it's already run spectacularly by Mr. Vincent."

"For your information," Luke said, "he's *my* dad, and I want *him* to run this school."

"I get that," Nicole said, nodding. "I mean, you're his son. But, do *you* want this school to be run by Mr. Vincent, Maddix?"

"Of course I do!" Maddix exclaimed. "He's my best friend's dad!"

"Is he your *only* friend?" Nicole asked, seemingly very interested in the floor at the moment.

"I—what?" Maddix looked at her, amazed at what she knew. "How do you know—?"

Nicole looked up, and smiled innocently."Context clues," she said. "I saw you and Luke walking to Mr. Vincent's office, remember? You looked like you wanted to know something. I know the way to Mr. Vincent's office. You were going in that direction. I saw earlier that you didn't talk to anyone but Luke the whole day. It's kind of obvious."

"What else do you know?" Luke asked.

"That you have been here your whole life," Nicole said.

"That's the most creepy thing I have ever heard," Luke said.

"You're wrong," Maddix said quietly.

"What?" Nicole said.

"What?" Luke said the same thing.

"I haven't been here my whole life," Maddix said. "I was taken."

Luke and Nicole's mouths dropped.

"What do you mean?" Luke asked.

"I was taken here as a baby," Maddix said. "I just realized. That dream was from the past. It really happened."

"It really happened?" Luke asked. Nicole didn't know what they were talking about.

"What really happened? What dream?"

Zennith's mouth dropped open. So he *knew*? From a *dream*? That was crazy. Zennith knew he had to strike, and soon. He needed him to think it was fake. Or that it was just a normal dream. Something. Anything. But he couldn't know the truth.

Night came, and as it did, Zennith prepared for what he was about to do.

The Raders were staying in a special room in Apollo Academy. So, in the dead of the night, they heard the windows rattle. Luke and Maddix heard it, too. Luke straightened up and said, "Wuzgoinon?"

"I don't know," Maddix said. They both looked at the windows and gasped. They were rattling so much, it was a wonder they weren't breaking! Suddenly, one of them opened—all by itself! Wind rushed into the room—but it wasn't windy outside. There was a growl, and Maddix and Luke ran out of the room. They threw open the first door they saw and hurried into what it yielded. There was a man, a woman, and a girl. It was Nicole and her parents.

"Where did *you* come from?" she said.

"N-nowhere," Luke replied. "Why?"

"Well, you kinda just shot right in here," Nicole said, "so you must've—"

BOOM.

The ceiling broke in half, and it fell on top of the kids and adults.

"Mom! Dad! Are you okay?" Nicole was screaming, trying to get out of the rubble. Someone gasped, and Nicole whipped around: Her mother was pointing at a man climbing into the room, having went through the window. Maddix and Luke emerged from the ceiling's debris. Maddix saw the man dressed in a cloak, and memories flashed back to him—that was the very man who had taken him to this school. He was tall, with darker hair than even Maddix's, and his brown eyes flashed dangerously through the scene. Zennith searched the room and found the boy. He said, "Nobody move, and I will make it stop." Everyone froze, and Zennith snapped his fingers. The fragments of the ceiling replaced themselves and all was silent. Zennith said, "Stay put. I only need one of you." Nicole's parents, Nicole herself, Maddix, and Luke stayed where they were. Luke looked at Maddix, whose hands were curled into fists.

"You," Zennith pointed at Maddix. "Come with me." Luke pushed Maddix, who stepped forward. Zennith was walking out of the room. Maddix, furious, followed.

CHAPTER 3
THE EXPLANATION

W hat do you want?" Maddix said angrily, watching Zennith as he created some sort of blue force field around them.

"I've got to tell you something."

"Why'd you do that?"

"Do what?"

"The force field thingy. Why'd you make it?"

"It's a Sound Field. I made it so that no one could hear our conversation."

"Okay. Well, if we can't be heard, I have some questions to ask you."

"Go ahead."

He knew the kid was wondering which question to ask first. After all these years, after all the secrets, after all the—well, everything!

"I know it was you who took me. Why'd you do it?"

Zennith hesitated. What should he tell the boy? Sidero had said, long ago: "If he asks you anything, tell him the truth, but not the full truth, understand? Tell him part of it, with little tweaks, but don't be flat-out lying." And Zennith had asked why he couldn't flat-out lie, but Sidero had said, "Questions will be answered in time, Zennith." How was Zennith to quickly think of a way to just say *part* of the truth, but not *all* of it?

"I was acting on orders."

"Whose?" Zennith knew the boy wasn't going to miss anything or leave anything he was wondering about out of the conversation.

"My master's."

"Who's your master?"

"He has a name I shall not speak of."

"What, are you scared of it?"

Zennith looked right into the boy's narrowed eyes and answered, "No, I am not scared of it."

"Why can't you mention it, then?"

"Because you will be very sorry if I did."

"Why?"

"Do you *really* want to waste time asking about my master, or do you have other questions?" Zennith knew he'd be able to switch the subject.

"Why did you take me?" he repeated the first question.

Zennith hesitated. He couldn't say, "I was acting on orders," again. Was the full truth best? *That's a stupid question*, he thought, *you know what Sidero told you. Not the full truth. Only half.* But, then again, why even *listen* to Sidero? *No, no, no*, Zennith mentally shook himself. *Don't get into trust and stuff. Just tell him to wake up. Maybe he'll think it's a dream.*

"Don't tell me to wake up." The boy's words startled Zennith. Could he read his mind?

"What?"

"Don't tell me to wake up," he repeated. "I know this is not a dream. Answer my question: Why did you take me?" Zennith turned to leave. He couldn't process this all at once. Even though it was only two questions, the questions themselves were complex. Question one: What should he answer the boy? Question two: Could he read minds?

"What are you doing?"

Zennith turned around to face him. He said, "I'm leaving. Isn't it obvious?"

"Why are you leaving?" Maddix said angrily. "You said you'd give me answers!" Zennith turned his back on him and left the Sound Field, leaving Maddix clenching his fists furiously.

CHAPTER 4
THE IDEA

Night air wafted through an empty classroom's window.

"Maddix, this isn't going to help," Nicole said for the fifth time. "As much as you might think so, sitting in an empty room in the middle of the night doesn't help with shock."

"For the last time," Luke said, "it's not shock, it's anger, and will you please be quiet? He's trying to think."

"Yes, but—"

"Shhhh!"

Maddix looked at the floor. He had heard of the phrase, 'too good to be true' before, but he'd never actually lived it. For a minute, he thought that he was finally going to get answers to questions that had been floating in his head for years, but Zennith had to ruin it.

Why'd he walk out on him like that? Was Maddix's one question unanswerable? Even though these thoughts were important, the thing that Maddix thought was most major was the fact that Maddix could see Zennith's thoughts. He never knew he could do this, so it came as a shock to him. One minute, he was facing Zennith, thinking, *What's the answer? Why isn't he answering me?* He made a face—a fierce one. And then, he saw dancing flames, and the next minute, he was facing numbers, letters, and images. The words, *Don't get into trust and stuff. Just tell him to wake up. Maybe he'll think it's a dream,* were displayed right in front of his eyes. A picture of a man Maddix recognized as Zennith was shaking the hand of a cloaked man, the hood covering his face. Maddix felt a sharp pain in his chest when he saw him. Suddenly, he had been looking at Zennith, the non-photographic Zennith, and the words escaped from his mouth.

"Don't tell me to wake up."

How did he get inside Zennith's mind? Was it the flames? And, speaking of the flames, how did they appear? Maddix thought, *I wasn't thinking about anything to do with fire. Maybe that's how I went into Zennith's mind! But how?*

Maddix explained his and Zennith's conversation and his thoughts to Luke in a low voice, not wanting Nicole to hear—but she did. Of course, she *was* about two feet away from them.

"Y'know, you could just go to the Power Analyzation building. We could go, too." Nicole said.

Luke turned to her. "Why would we take *you* with us? You're not our friend or anything."

Nicole glared at him; of course she was their friend—why else would she be with them in the middle of the night? "I meant that he could take us with him because we need to. A law was passed in the Office of General Magic, or OGM, that each child showing magical activity should go to the Power Analyzation to be analyzed."

"It sounds like you've memorized the law," Luke said.

"Does it?" Nicole replied. "Actually, I was studying the OGM with my dad once, and he told me that all rules are important."

Luke rolled his eyes and asked, "So, how are we gonna get there? Will our parents take us?"

"Yeah," Nicole answered. "At least, mine will. But I don't know about your dad, Luke. Is he too fussed about laws?"

Luke bared his teeth. "You are such a—"

"Calm down!" Maddix exclaimed. "Let's just ask about the Power Analyzation tomorrow." And, with that, he left the room.

"The next morning, Maddix and Luke hurried to Nicole's room, where they found Nicole herself looking out the window.

"What are you staring at?" Luke demanded.

Nicole whipped around. "Nothing," she said. Luke and Maddix looked out the window and saw Nicole's parents talking to Luke's dad.

"What are they talking about?" Maddix asked.

"No doubt the school's gonna be run by my dad now," Nicole whispered.

"You should be dancing on the ceiling, then," Luke snarled. "Why are you so sad? This is what you've been wanting, isn't it?"

Nicole shook her head. "No. I'm mean, yes. But not anymore."

"Why?" Maddix asked.

"Why do you think?" Nicole exploded. She stood up and started pacing the room. "After that—that weird man broke into this room, I want you to stay here!"

"Why?" Luke asked.

"To investigate!" Nicole threw her hands into the air, as if Luke and Maddix were driving her insane. "I am *not* about do it all myself. Boys these days." She clapped her hand to her forehead and shook her head. Although she sounded like that was the whole reason, Maddix felt there was more to the story.

"Nicole," Luke said, not understanding why she was so mad all of a sudden, "calm down. We can make sure your dad doesn't take over and kick us out."

"Do you have any idea?" Nicole asked him.

"I have an idea," Maddix said. "Let's go to Power Analyzation."

CHAPTER 5
DISAPPOINTMENT

Y ou WHAT?"

"I know it doesn't sound good, but I'll make sure it happens next time." Zennith had just reported that he hadn't put the tracking device on the boy. Sidero was enraged, as expected.

"'Next time'?" Sidero laughed. "You think there's going to be a 'next time' after what you did? I was trusting you, Zennith. You are my most faithful servant, and you blew it!"

"I'm sure we'll get another chance," Zennith said confidently, though not believing it himself.

"But now the boy knows who you *are*, what you *look like*, everything! There is NOT going to be another chance!" Breathing fast, fists clenched, his face right up close to Zennith's, Sidero started to think. What if...?

"However," he said, in a much calmer voice, "if you make a signature—I don't know—sound, you could do it during the *day*. Because, of course they would expect you to do it at night. And also, I created this." He held up a miniscule chip. "This can also enable us to hear every conversation he has, and record it. And it makes the tracking device as tiny as this is." Sidero put the chip into the tracking device, pushed a few buttons, and the tracking device/conversation recorder was as minute as the conversation recorder was alone.

"Brilliant," Zennith pocketed it. Then, he remembered Parker going into his mind.

"Sidero," Zennith said, "the boy—does he have any powers?"

"Powers?" Sidero repeated. "I should think not. Why?"

"Well, sir, he—went into my mind."

Sidero, trying to hide that he was impressed, said, "Oh, yes. There's that part."

"'That part'?" Zennith asked. "What are you not telling me, Sidero?"

"Well," Sidero wrung his hands; he looked uncomfortable, "when we took him to that tower, I noticed some—er—weird things happening."

"What weird things?" Zennith said.

"Weird things like," Sidero said, "a strange look on his face."

"So?" Zennith asked. "Everyone can have a strange look on their face. What was so special about his?"

"Well," Sidero responded, "it was like his face was saying, 'There's something about to happen, and you're not gonna like it.' And then, he went into my mind."

"So, after he gave you that Dislike What's About to Happen face, he went into your mind? Only after that?" Zennith said.

"Yes, only after the DWAH face," Sidero replied. "You think that's special?"

"Of course I do!" Zennith exclaimed. "I think that everything the boy did to you was special, too! Don't you see? This boy could be a much more dangerous threat than we've ever imagined. My only question is: why didn't you tell me this before?"

"Weakness, Zennith," Sidero admitted. "It would show that I was too weak to keep my mind from him. What if you told the rest of the clan? I expect it would be a good joke for the McRathers."

"I am loyal to you," Zennith assured him, "I would never share the secrets you want me to keep."

"Yes, yes, yes," Sidero waved a hand. Suddenly, he had an idea. He smirked. "Zennith, what if we could have someone be at the school, to be our eyes and ears in *addition* to the tracking device?"

Knowing his master was in a thinking mode, Zennith did not ask why it would be in addition to the tracking device. If the person would be their eyes and ears, the tracking device wouldn't be needed, would it?

"But who?" Zennith asked instead.

"Let me think," Sidero said. "Who was—or maybe still is—loyal to me? Ah, of course!" Rubbing his hands together, he said, "Send a message to Lucian Dagner."

CHAPTER 6
THE ANTIQUE SHOP

Nicole trotted up to her father in the room where her family was staying and asked, "Dad, have we been to the Power Analyzation building?"

"I just hope Nicole pulls it off," Luke hissed to Maddix as they hid behind one of the armchairs. It had been Nicole's idea: While she would go and ask her dad if she could go to the Power Analyzation, Maddix and Luke would hide. And if her father said yes, she would say that a couple of her friends would like to come. ("But you know we're not your friends, right?" an annoyed Luke asked). But, she would only say this at the last minute. Then, Luke and Maddix would come. ("But you two have to act polite, my dad has to like you," Nicole said. Luke had muttered to Maddix, "We didn't make much of a first impression, though. I don't think he would like us even if we acted as polite as we could possibly be.") Also, Nicole would ask her father, and if he said yes, she'd distract him while Luke and Maddix went out of the room. And, if he said no, Nicole "would beg and beg, because he'd do *anything* for me if I do that."

"The Power Analyzation building?" Mr. Rader asked presently.

"Yes," Nicole nodded. She spoke the same words that she had said to Maddix and Luke the night before: "A law was passed in the Office of General Magic, or OGM, that each child showing magical activity should go to the Power Analyzation to be analyzed." Her father didn't look at all surprised that his daughter had practically memorized the law.

"Alright," he said, "but only because it is an Office of General Magic law. I think we can go in a couple of hours."

"A couple of hours?" Nicole echoed. "Why can't we go now?"

"I've got a meeting with Mr. Vincent," Mr. Rader said. "And then I have to finish up some work."

"Okay," Nicole replied. "Wait, where's your computer? You might need it for your work later."

"Why would you ask that?" Mr. Rader asked suspiciously. "Did you hide it again?"

"Maybe I hid it over there," Nicole smiled guiltily. She pointed to the other side of the room. Maddix guessed

Nicole hid her father's computer a lot; Mr. Rader didn't look angry.

While Mr. Rader was looking where Nicole had pointed, Nicole herself motioned to Luke and Maddix. They crept to the door, opened it silently, and slipped out. Nicole closed the door in equal silence and said, "I was just joking, Dad. I didn't hide it!"

Two hours later, Mr. Rader approached his daughter outside the school.

"Okay, we can go now," he said. Nicole grinned at him.

When they were standing by their car, Nicole said to her father, "Oh, I forgot—a couple of my friends were coming, too. They heard what we were doing and they wanted to come. Can I go get them?" Mr. Rader nodded slowly, and Nicole ran to Luke and Maddix's room.

"It's time to go," she panted. Luke went to his dad and told him that they were going to the Power Analyzation building. Mr. Vincent replied with a shrug, not looking up from the book he was reading. As Maddix, Luke, and Nicole left the room, Nicole told them that her father had had a meeting with Luke's.

"I don't think it went well," Nicole said, "for Mr. Vincent, anyway. I'm sorry," she added, seeing Luke's face.

"All the more reason we should do this," Maddix said. "What if we *have* powers? We can use them to save the school!" Nicole and Luke nodded.

"Wouldn't it be cool to have superpowers?" Luke said. "Like, if you could fly, you could just—"

"Actually," Nicole interrupted, "the powers you have—that is, if you even have them—are not superpowers. There's a difference between superpowers and magical powers. In the magical world, powers are a big deal. If you go to the Power Analyzation building and your results are that you have powers, you go for further testing. Of course, the type of power does make a difference. For instance, if you have the power of teleportation, you will not have as much additional testing as if you have any elemental powers."

"How do you know all this stuff, anyway?" Luke asked her.

"I studied with my dad, remember?" she said. "And, the real question is, how do you *not* know? Don't you guys work here?"

"Wait, wait, wait, back up," Maddix said. "Did you say, 'further testing'?"

"Yes," Nicole nodded, turning away from Luke. "Thank you for stopping me, actually, I forgot something about that. There's an exception for further testing: if you have a more—how do I put this?—*powerful* power, then you skip the further testing and go straight to Exercises and Control, which is usually *after* the further testing. In Exercises and Control, you will try to harness your powers and—let's say—*experiment* with them."

"Okay," Luke said. "Are you finished?"

"Nope," Nicole responded. "There are rules to powers, too. The most important rule is: you can't use your powers until you're a certain age, *unless* you're in a life-threatening situation."

"What age do you have to be?" Luke asked.

"Sixteen," Nicole answered.

"*Sixteen?*" Maddix repeated.

"Yes," Nicole said. "If you're wondering about that, the reason—"

"For Pete's sake, Nicole!" Luke exploded. "Please, shut up for once!"

"You know, you'll regret that in five years' time," Nicole replied, rolling up her sleeves.

Luke hesitated, and then started to speak, but Nicole cut him off.

"I'll be sixteen in five years, doofus!" she exclaimed. "I'll use my powers—"

"Your powers?" Luke repeated. "*Your powers?* How do you know you even *have* powers?"

Maddix, who had kept quiet in hoping that they would work it out themselves, decided to speak up.

"Break it up, guys. And we should probably figure out the rest of the plan..."

"What rest of the plan?" Nicole asked. "I mean, we get in, we get analyzed, we go."

"But what about the details?" Maddix said. "What if we have powers and we have to go through further testing? Or one of us has—using your words—more powerful powers and has to go straight to Exercises and Control—"

"Then we'll wait for them," Nicole responded. "It usually doesn't take that long. Also, there are three stages to the Power Analyzation Test: the normal test, further testing, and Exercises and Control. You have to go to Exercises and Control anyway, it's just that the one of us with more powerful powers would go sooner."

"Well, it wasn't as bad as the lecture about the difference between superpowers and magical powers." Luke whispered to Maddix.

They had finally reached the car.

"Why'd it take you so long?" Mr. Rader asked, obviously as politely as he could. Maddix thought about this, and didn't know what to think of it.

"Ready?" Nicole asked her father. He nodded. Maddix, Luke, Nicole, and Mr. Rader got into the car. Soon, they were off.

A few minutes later, they stopped in front of a large, brick building. Maddix whispered to Nicole, "Is this the Power Analyzation building?"

"Yes," Nicole replied, "but it's disguised as an antique shop."

"Why would an antique shop be so big?" Maddix asked her.

"I don't know," she answered. "One time, I saw a woman ask the store manager that, and he said, 'We have a lot of antiques. Now, if you'll excuse me, I need to get something in the back.' And the woman never went there again."

Maddix wondered how she knew that last part.

"What are you whispering about?" Luke asked.

"Why that 'antique shop' is so big," Maddix said.

"Oh," Luke nodded.

"You know about the disguise?" Nicole asked.

"Yeah!" Luke said. "Why are you so surprised? I know stuff!"

"Keep it down," Nicole said. "We're parking."

A moment later, Mr. Rader, Nicole, Luke, and Maddix entered the shop.

"Hello," Mr. Rader said to the man at the counter, "My name is Daniel Rader. I'm here for *powerful* business."

The man's face turned serious. He nodded and asked, "You're here for the... test?"

Mr. Rader said, "Yes. I am here for the Power Analyzation test for one—" Nicole looked at him "—three people."

"My name is Aaron Taylor," the man said, "and I need you to come to the back with me." Taylor led them into the back, where there was small bottle lying on a table. Maddix spotted this first because it was the only small thing. There were large buckets and pails and old grandfather clocks and a lot of other ancient things.

"Hand on bottle," Taylor said. Nicole, Maddix, Luke, Mr. Rader, and Taylor place their hands on the small bottle.

"*Mira Sinto!*" Taylor exclaimed, and there was a flash of purple, and they were standing somewhere else.

CHAPTER 7
GRIFFIN CALLING

"You sure Sirien's up to the job? You're quite sure?"
Zennith wanted to know.

"Well, if he wasn't, he wouldn't be doing it now, would he? And he's doing a fine job."

Zennith nodded. Sidero was right. Sirien was doing a spectacular job: no one suspected a thing. And putting the real Mr. Rader in the East tower was a perfect place to hide him; no one's been there for years.

"I wonder what he's doing now?" Sidero said. "He might be luring them into his trap by now; we'll see what happens."

"And he told me that Rader literally went up to him and *asked* to go to the Power Analyzation room. I mean, how absurd was that?"

Sidero nodded. "I know. She's walking right into our trap."

"And he was even going to ask her, 'Hello, Nicole. Would you like to go to Power Analyzation with me? The law says you have to.' But she went up to *ask* him right before he was going to do so himself!"

Sidero looked at Zennith. He sure was happy about this.

"Feel happy now," Sidero said darkly, "because we may have a *lot* of problems coming up."

Zennith's face turned serious. He nodded. "Don't you think, of all people, that *I* would be aware of that?"

CHAPTER 8
POWER ANALYZATION

That "somewhere else" was a simple, white room. The only things in it were about ten chairs and a couple tables.

"This is the Power Analyzation waiting room," Mr. Rader said. Maddix looked around: Taylor was gone.

"Where's Taylor?" Luke voiced what Maddix was wondering.

"Back to the antique shop," Nicole said. She looked at him, almost with a sense of pity. "But… you should know that, shouldn't you?"

"What do you mean?" Luke asked.

"I mean," Nicole responded, "you're connected with magic. Don't you know about the Teleportation System?"

"Teleportation System?" Luke repeated. "I only know that the Power Analyzation building is disguised as an antique shop, and that you can somehow get to the Power Analyzation part from the back room!"

"Really?" Nicole said. "I would've thought—"

"Cut it for now, guys," Maddix interrupted. "We need to focus on what's happening."

"Right," Luke nodded. He turned to Mr. Rader. "Nicole's d—I mean, sir, where to from here?"

"We wait," Mr. Rader replied. "And I'm glad at least one Vincent's got their manners right." Nicole smiled at a bewildered Luke, who wondered why Mr. Rader had insulted his father for no reason.

A woman, clipboard in hand, entered the waiting room and approached Mr. Rader. "Do you have an appointment, sir?"

"No," Mr. Rader answered, "but I have three children who need to take the Power Analyzation Test."

"Okay, then," the woman consulted the clipboard. "You're in luck, not many people came today for the Test. May I ask your name?"

"Daniel Rader," he said.

"May I have the children's names and ages?" the woman asked.

"Nicole Rader," Mr. Rader answered, "Luke Vincent, and Maddix Parker. They're all eleven." The woman thanked him and disappeared into the hallway.

A few moments later, sure enough, the woman was back.

"Can I see the youngest?"

"I was born on March 8," Luke said.

"May 19," Nicole said.

"November 30," Maddix said, titling his head to the left to indicate that he meant the previous year. Nicole went first into a room marked 3.

"Each Test takes about three minutes," the woman told them. Luke and Maddix tried to look through the windows, but an angry Mr. Rader grabbed them and carried them away.

"Did I mention that the Power Analyzation Test was supposed to be *not watched*?" he said through gritted teeth.

Nicole came out of the room, grinning from ear-to-ear.

"What powers?" Luke asked.

"Super Hearing," Nicole replied. Luke was next in room eight.

He came out minutes later. Maddix asked what powers he had.

"Invisibility," Luke responded. Maddix went into room twelve. Everything was white: the walls, the floor, everything. Even the dentist's chair in the middle. Maddix sat in it, and the woman introduced herself as Dr. Raina Helmer.

"You've got to be Maddix, right?"

Maddix nodded.

"Okay, so we're going to see how you react to things," she said. Dr. Helmer went to a desk and took out a sort of ray gun.

"Is this really necessary?" Maddix asked nervously.

"Yes, it's basically the whole test," Helmer answered, pushing some buttons.

"Will it kill me?" Maddix said.

"Of course not," Helmer responded, "it just might knock you out."

"*What?*" Maddix was scared; what if it knocked him out?

"Three, two, one," Helmer said, and she pushed the ON button. There was a blue ray of light, and Maddix jumped out of the chair.

"Oops," Helmer said, "sorry. Sometimes it goes off on its own. There we go. Ready yourself, now. And—go!" She flipped a switch, and there was a green ray of light. Maddix instinctively (but, it seemed, stupidly) gave it a face, and saw dancing flames. But, this time, the flames flickered and died. He somehow deflected the ray. He clutched his head.

"Whoa," Helmer grinned. "*That* was impressive. I haven't seen anyone do that in years."

"Do what?" Maddix asked.

"You can read minds, Maddix!" Helmer exclaimed.

"How did you get reading minds from me somehow deflecting a ray of light?"

"What did you do *before* you deflected it, though?" Helmer asked excitedly.

"I made a face," Maddix replied. "But what's that got to do with—"

"Don't you see?" Helmer burst out. "You made the famous DWAH face—Dislike What's About to Happen—and you blocked the ray! Did you see anything before you blocked it?"

"Yeah," Maddix responded, "fire. But it died."

"Because," Helmer explained, "you had no mind to go into."

"Go into?" Maddix repeated. "I thought you said I could only read minds!"

"Well, it's kind of the same thing," Helmer told him. "If you could read a person's mind, you could see what they're thinking. And if you go into a person's mind, you could see what they were thinking as well. But, if you go into someone's mind, you could see what they were thinking in the past, what they've done, and what they're thinking presently."

"That's *so* cool!" Maddix exclaimed. But then, something hit him: what if he couldn't control it, and something bad happened? "But, I have a question: what if I can't control it?"

"All things will be taken care of," Helmer reassured him. "Now, come on, we've got to get back to the waiting room."

As soon as Maddix exited room twelve, Luke and Nicole asked, "What powers do you have?"

"Mind reading," Maddix replied. Nicole mouthed, "Of course!"

"So, we have to go to further testing now," Helmer said. She turned to Mr. Rader. "I'll be back in just a minute." She left. Mr. Rader turned to Maddix. "Could I see you for a second?" He opened the door of a nearby closet. Maddix shrugged and said, "Okay." Mr. Rader shut the door behind Maddix as he entered.

"What is it?" Maddix asked.

"What is it, you ask?" came a rasping voice. Maddix realized it was coming from Mr. Rader's mouth. "Well, there are a lot of things that are 'it,' Parker. But right now, I want to address only one of them." Maddix looked fearfully at Mr. Rader—but there wasn't Mr. Rader anymore. A tall, scary creature stood before him. It had the body of a lion, and the feet, wings, and head of an eagle. It was a griffin. Maddix was frozen with fear.

"My master will be pleased with me," he said. "I, Malachi Sirien, have succeeded in capturing Sidero's greatest enemy! I will be praised beyond my wildest dreams! The father of a silly girl is locked up in the East tower, for I have taken his place! Humans can be so stupid these days."

Sidero... so *that* was Zennith's master's name! Maddix thought, *This guy* has *to be on Zennith's side—which is a bad one—so I need some backup.*

"Help!" Maddix screamed. "I need help! Somebody! Please!" The closet door came crashing down, revealing Luke and Nicole.

"Guys!" Maddix yelled. "Help me!"

"I didn't need Super Hearing to hear you shouting!" Nicole hollered. "But I did need it to hear that other voice! I bet it was him!"

"Where's your dad?" Luke asked Nicole.

"Probably hiding somewhere," Nicole replied. "He's not much of a fighter!"

"You're dad's locked up!" Maddix exclaimed. Nicole looked at him like he was crazy.

"What?"

"I'm serious!" Maddix said. "This guy replaced your dad—he's an imposter, who turned into a griffin! Now how are we going to fight him?"

"Are you nuts?" Nicole hollered. "I can't fight my dad!"

"He's *not* your dad!" Luke said. "Didn't you hear him? Your dad's locked up somewhere else!"

Nicole looked like she was at a loss for words. Inexplicably, she said, "Don't kill him!"

"I can't count on that!" Luke ran up to the griffin and tried to punch him in the nose, but Sirien lazily put up his claw and sent Luke crashing down to the floor.

"We can't fight in a closet!" Luke exclaimed, rubbing his head.

"You are right about the closet part," Sirien said. He kicked the door, and it broke clean off its hinges, "but not about the fight." He made a grab for Maddix, who ducked.

"We need to get you out of here, Maddix!" Nicole called.

"You're not getting out," Sirien said. "At least, not without me."

Maddix was too busy contemplating his words to notice that the griffin was attempting to grab him again. This time, he succeeded. Maddix thought, *I can use my powers. But I can't control them! What if it doesn't work, what if it hurts Luke or Nicole, what if this whole place comes crashing down?*

Maddix started breathing quickly. And then, he felt angry all of a sudden. *This guy messes with me, he messes with my powers.* He focused on stopping Sirien. He closed his eyes, and, to his delight, he saw dancing flames. He looked into Sirien's beady eyes, and made a face. It was called the DWAH face, apparently—the Dislike What's About to Happen face—and it was his specialty.

He opened his eyes, and he was looking at letters and numbers—just like Zennith's mind, but much more angry. But how could a mind be angry? There were a bunch of thoughts in there, like, *I need to impress my master. I need to fulfill my master's wishes. I need to capture Maddix Parker. I need to* NOW!

Maddix, knowing he only had seconds—because he didn't have much control—searched the thoughts for something useful. There—*No one knows my weakness. I need to keep it a secret that I can be defeated by one touching my weak spot: under my left wing.*

Maddix thought, *What dummy puts their weakness in an unprotected mind?* And then he realized that *everybody* probably did that—except maybe Sidero. A second later, Maddix was back in Sirien's claw. Luckily, he was in his left claw. If Sirien started to fly, of course he would flap his wings—so Maddix would have an opening! Sure enough, Sirien made his move a moment later, and flapped his wings slowly. Maddix squirmed and struggled, until he could finally free his right arm. He punched under Sirien's left wing as the griffin flapped his wings again. Sirien howled, "Owwww!"

At that moment, Maddix was dropped. Fortunately, he was only a few feet off the ground. Nicole and Luke rushed to him as a bunch of men in black suits started wrestling Sirien.

"Maddix, are you okay?" Nicole asked.

"Get away from him, you traitor," Luke snarled.

"I'm not a traitor!" Nicole exclaimed. "Luke, please, I didn't know about my dad!"

"I heard him say something about Nicole's father being locked up, remember?" Maddix said. "He's in the East tower." He turned to Luke. "She's not a traitor, Luke. How could she have known that her father was kidnapped and replaced by a griffin?"

"Did you catch his name, Maddix?" Nicole asked. "Just asking. It might be useful."

"Of course he didn't get his name!" Luke exclaimed. "He couldn't just ask, 'hey, dude, can I have your name? I need it to defeat you.' Seriously, Nicole?"

"I actually got his name," Maddix said, "Malachi Sirien."

"I know that name!" Nicole said. "My dad told me that Malachi Sirien was a griffin that escaped from a sort of magical circus. Some say he came across some 'evil master' and became loyal to him, helping him destroy things all over the place."

"That makes sense!" Maddix exclaimed. "He said something like, 'my master will be pleased with me.' And also something like, 'I have succeeded in capturing Sidero's greatest enemy!' I think he was talking about me."

"Sidero!" Nicole jumped up. "He's the most feared, evil, and powerful enchanter of all time!"

"Enchanter?" Maddix repeated. "What's that?"

"It's kind of like a wizard," Nicole explained. "An enchanter is a male person who can do magic, and an enchantress is a female person who can do magic."

"Okay," Maddix said.

"Guys," Luke said, "have you got any more information on Sidero?"

"Yeah," Nicole replied. "Maddix is apparently his greatest enemy."

"How can I be an extremely powerful enchanter's greatest enemy?" Maddix asked. "I'm just a kid!"

"A kid with awesome powers!" Luke said. "Maddix, you've got to stop him from doing any more damage."

"What?" Maddix said. "No, you can't be serious."

"It's your destiny, Maddix." Nicole looked at him. "I'm serious."

CHAPTER 9
THE TROUBLE WITH TEACHERS

M addix and Luke searched the East tower a half hour later, after Aaron Taylor safely teleported them back, and they had stopped at Mr. Vincent's office to grab a ring of keys. Nicole didn't want to come, because she "couldn't handle seeing her dad weak."

Of course, the door was locked.

"If Nicole were here, she could use her powers to try to hear if there was any movement inside," Maddix said. "That way, we could've made sure it wasn't a trap and not open the door."

"Yeah, but Nicole's not here," Luke said. "So stop thinking about it." Maddix was taken aback.

"Are you angry about something?" he asked.

"No," Luke responded, "it's just—what if Nicole lied?"

"What do you mean?"

"What if she knew that her dad was kidnapped and replaced by an evil griffin?"

"She would've told us about it. Don't you think Nicole would use her common sense—"

"But what if she was on his side?"

"Luke—"

"We don't even know her that well! Maddix, think of the things that have happened. If there's anything we've learned, it's that nothing is impossible! And, in this case, it's a bad thing! Anything could happen."

Maddix looked at his best friend. What if he was right?

"If it makes you happy," Maddix said, "we'll have her tested for lies when we question her about it."

Luke nodded. "Thanks."

Maddix tried out each key on the ring until he heard the satisfying click. They opened the door and looked around.

Suddenly, they heard a scuffle. Maddix and Luke whipped around. There, lying on the floor, was a bound man. He had a black eye; Maddix guessed that the real Mr. Rader had put up a fight with the fake one.

"Are you Daniel Rader?" Luke asked nervously. The man nodded his head vigorously. Maddix and Luke dropped to the ground and untied him.

"What happened?" he gasped. "Where's the flying lion?"

"The griffin?" Maddix said. "He's been taken away."

"The good 'taken away?'" Mr. Rader asked.

Luke nodded. "Are you okay?"

"Yes," he replied. "Well, kind of. I just have this." He pointed to the black eye. "And it's not that bad. Where's Nicole? And Melissa?"

"Who's Melissa?" Luke asked.

"My wife," Mr. Rader said. "Can you please tell me where Nicole is now?"

"She's safe," Maddix told him. "They're both safe. We were just with Nicole, and she was on the phone with her mom."

"Good," Mr. Rader said. "Oh, thank heavens!"

"I have a question," Luke said. "Why did you want to take over this place?"

"Take over?" Mr. Rader repeated. "My dear boy, I wouldn't take over *this* place! Mr. Vincent runs it splendidly!"

Luke nodded, pleased.

Mr. Rader said, "Thank you for untying me."

"No problem," Luke said. "Now, if you'll come with us…" Luke, Maddix, and Mr. Rader ran down the tower's staircase and across the courtyard. They ran into the building, and into Mr. Vincent's office. Nicole was there, as well as Mr. Vincent himself. When Nicole saw her father, she ran to him and they hugged.

"Dad!" Nicole exclaimed. "My real dad! I'm so glad you're alive!"

"Forget me," Mr. Rader said, "I thought *you* were surely dead, with that griffin running about!"

"Hello," Mr. Vincent shook hands with Mr. Rader.

"Dad, the real Mr. Rader doesn't have any interest in taking over this place," Luke told his father. "So we can keep Apollo Academy!"

"That's great news!" Mr. Vincent exclaimed.

"I was convinced since my first day here that everything was fine," Mr. Rader said. "So, since we have no business here, I think me, Nicole, and my wife need to head home."

They were almost out the door when Luke suddenly had an idea.

"Can Nicole attend Apollo Academy?"

"Really, Luke," Mr. Vincent said, "I think that's a little too—"

"That would be *awesome*!" Nicole exclaimed. She turned to her father. "Dad, can't I go? I've been here for awhile and it's *really* cool."

"I think your mother—" Mr. Rader began.

"Would like to have me come here," Nicole said. "She's always been saying that I needed a better education than at my other school. This is a great opportunity!"

"I really think—" Mr. Rader said.

"Please?" Maddix, Luke, and Nicole begged.

"Oh, fine," Mr. Rader said finally. "I think you'll be in good hands."

"YES!" the three children shouted.

"Well, I'd best be off," Mr. Rader said. "Bye, Nicole!" He hugged his daughter and went out the door.

"Why did you ask for me to stay?" Nicole asked Luke. "I thought that you thought I was a traitor."

"I just had this—feeling," Luke told her, "that you were telling the truth. And, after all we've been through, I think you've earned being our friend." Nicole glowed.

"Thanks, Luke."

"No problem."

Nicole settled into Apollo in the next few days. Maddix and Luke were happy to have her around; they laughed after classes and talked during lunch. Mr. Vincent said that Maddix and Luke could take the notes of all the classes Nicole was in at the same time she was in them. Things were going well, until one particular Friday afternoon when Mr. Vincent brought them into an empty classroom to talk.

"I would like to introduce a new teacher to you," Mr. Vincent said to Maddix, Luke, and Nicole. He indicated a tall man with sleek, black hair and a smirk. "This is Mr. Lucian Dagner. He will be teaching Mythology."

"I thought Mrs. Gilders was teaching that," Maddix said.

"Lori didn't seem fit to teach that subject anymore," Dagner said, "so she has been demoted to Ancient Artifacts of History."

"But that's the class half the students skip!" Luke exclaimed. "So Mr. Landers, the teacher, quit."

"Things happen," Dagner replied. "That's how life is."

Luke turned to his dad. "Father, may I have a word with you?"

"Sure," Mr. Vincent said. Luke took his dad outside, leaving Maddix and Nicole alone with Dagner.

"We'll go with them," Maddix said, starting to run off, but Dagner grabbed his hand.

"I think it's a rather private conversation, Parker," he said.

"How do you know my name?" Maddix asked.

"Use your common sense," Dagner said. "Would Mr. Vincent have told me your names?"

"I guess so," Maddix said. Dagner nodded.

Meanwhile, out in the hallway, Luke was discussing Dagner with his father.

"He gives me the creeps, Dad!" he exclaimed. "And he looks evil. E-V-I-L. Evil."

"Luke, you can't be serious," Mr. Vincent responded. "Lucian is the perfect fit for the job."

"Maybe he is," Luke said, "but he kept looking at Maddix, and Dad, there was something in his eyes—when he looked at Maddix the way he did, I just know he's not on our side!"

"Luke, calm down," Mr. Vincent said. "You may be a little paranoid because of Sirien. There's nothing to worry about."

"Dad, if you'll just listen—"

"I've heard enough. If you say one more word about Lucian being evil—"

Just then, Nicole opened the door.

"I couldn't help overhearing your conversation," she said, "and I think Luke's right. Well, maybe not *fully* right to you, Mr. Vincent, but could you just keep an eye on Dagner? We... we wouldn't keep pestering you about him if you did."

"I bet you could help overhearing our conversation, Nicole," Mr. Vincent said. "Just because you have Super Hearing doesn't mean you can use it all the time."

"Sorry, Mr. Vincent," Nicole said, realizing that an adult—who usually was fairly kind to her—had just told her off. "Can you go back inside, please? Maddix is left in there with Dagner, and I don't think it's going too well."

She was right; while Nicole had escaped Dagner and talked with Luke and Mr. Vincent, Maddix and Dagner had just stared at each other. It had been *very* awkward. Maddix hadn't liked staring into those cold, gray eyes.

After Luke, Nicole, and Mr. Vincent were back inside, Dagner spoke.

"Mr. Vincent, can I request something?"

"Yes, of course," Mr. Vincent replied.

"In private?" Dagner eyed Luke, Maddix, and Nicole.

"Okay," Mr. Vincent then turned to the children. "Maddix, Luke, Nicole—leave us for a minute. And Nicole, I forbid you to use your powers. If you do, there will be punishment."

"He's a bit stern today, isn't he?" Nicole asked as they walked out of the office.

"Yeah, a bit," Luke said. "Dad's only stern when he's a little nervous."

"I'd be nervous," Maddix said. "With a guy like Dagner around, anxiety would be my full-time emotion." Maddix told him about Dagner grabbing his arm.

"And then he said for me to use my senses and ask myself if Mr. Vincent had told him my name. It was *way* too creepy to handle. Dagner's evil."

"That's what I was trying to tell my dad!" Luke exclaimed. "I even spelled it out for him, but he wouldn't listen. He kept saying that Dagner's a good guy."

"And I asked to keep an eye on him," Nicole said. "Dagner—more like Danger, if you ask me."

"Hey, Nicole," Luke said, "could you use your powers to hear their conversation?"

"You heard what your father said—"

"I know what my dad said, but it would be a good opportunity to see if Dagner's an evil guy. What if he was threatening my dad right now?"

"It might be a little late. We wouldn't hear their full conversation."

"Who cares? All we need is a bit."

Luke had a look in his eye that said, "Come on, let's do some trouble for once." Maddix half liked it, half hated it.

"Alright, I'll do it," Nicole gave in. "But how will you hear it?"

"Say it as you hear it," Luke said.

"Okay," Nicole screwed up her face and then said what she heard. Maddix wrote it down quickly in a notebook.

"Really, Mr. Vincent, I think this is a good choice," Dagner said.

"Are you sure?" Mr. Vincent asked. "I don't think he'll like it."

"He'll be fine. Hasn't he dealt with things he doesn't like before?" Dagner said. "Let me keep an eye on Parker, it'll make security so much easier. I'm always in the places he is."

"And you're sure this will work?" Mr. Vincent asked uncertainly.

"Positive," Dagner responded.

"Well, I guess we better get Maddix, Luke, and Nicole back in here." Mr. Vincent said.

"Just one more thing: you're not telling Parker about this, are you?" Dagner said.

"Maddix? No, of course not. And, if Nicole's kept her promise, he won't know

about it. We're good." Mr. Vincent ended the conversation.

Mr. Vincent himself opened the classroom door, and Maddix hastily shoved the notebook in his pocket. He saw Nicole screw up her face and turn her powers off. Unfortunately, so did Mr. Vincent.

"Is something wrong, Nicole?" he asked.

"No," Nicole replied. "I-I was just thinking of a question Mr. Willington asked in class today." Maddix liked how quickly Nicole thought of lies.

"Interesting," Dagner said. "You're sure you weren't doing anything else, Rader?'"

"I'm completely sure," Nicole replied with conviction.

"Come on, now, you don't want to be late for your first lesson." Mr. Vincent said, leading Nicole, Maddix, and Luke down the hallway. Dagner smirked, pleased with himself.

Maddix showed Luke and Nicole what he wrote.

"Why'd you write in cursive?" Luke asked. "I *never* see you write in cursive!"

"I write in cursive when I'm scared," Maddix said. "What can I say?"

CHAPTER 10
CONFIRMATION

L ucian got our message, I presume?" Sidero asked his servant.

    He had been waiting all day to know what Zennith was so keen to discuss. Of course, he didn't want to show his interest. What if someone saw that Sidero, the great and powerful, was showing an interest in conversing with someone who was lower than him?

    Sidero looked to the skies. Dark clouds gathered around the tall, secluded hill in which he and Zennith were standing. To Sidero, dark clouds were a good sign, especially at night.

    "Yes," Zennith said presently. "He rose to the occasion magnificently."

    "Will he keep an eye on the Parker boy?" Sidero asked.

"He's just contacted me," Zennith said. Sidero's heart jumped; this was what he'd been waiting to hear.

"And he will," Zennith said. "He's got permission from that Will Vincent."

"Ah, Lucian," Sidero said, "always asking for permission. But, of course, if he hadn't, it would look very suspicious. Even a man like Vincent would think something's up."

"What is Lucian up to these days, anyway?" Zennith asked. "You know, before we communicated with him?"

"He's been studying Torture Principles," Sidero said, looking at his fingers. "And I recently heard that he was reading a book called, *Sneak Attacks: How to Master the Element of Surprise.*"

"Sounds like he's the man for the job, then?" Zennith said.

Sidero nodded. "He said when he contacted back, '*Don't worry, I'll do it. You can count on me, Sidero. As you know, I have been working on all things malicious.*' Leave it up to Lucian to use 'malicious' in the way he did."

"That man is sometimes insane, though," Zennith said. "I mean, that snarl of his! You'd think *I* was his enemy!"

"His snarl and his sneer," Sidero said. "Yes."

"You sound like you are going to do something professional right about now." Zennith said, eyeing him.

The Firecatcher

Sidero said, sounding very professional, "And some of the best of us gaze upon the horizons, wistfully thinking how life would be—"

"You know, sometimes you scare me," Zennith said, as if talking to an old friend. "Your methods are very interesting."

"How I do things," Sidero said, staying professional. "Yes, a life mystery. Wonder, listen, think—"

"Okay, now I think you're quoting," Zennith said. "Are you quoting from something?"

"No," Sidero said, not wanting to say that he was speaking made-up, important-sounding words.

"Riiiight," Zennith muttered as he looked away.

The clouds suddenly turned a pearly white. Sidero looked up.

"The dawn is upon us," he said. "Night leaves us, so we should leave this hill." And, with that, the two beings disappeared from sight.

70

CHAPTER 11
F IS FOR FOOLISH

A blood-red sun started to sink in the sky. Maddix looked out his bedroom window, wondering how the next day would play out. He wasn't looking forward to it at all.

"Maddix," Mr. Vincent had told him today, "this year, we are studying mirrors. Nicole requested that you and Luke accompany her on a field trip in Mythology class. The students will be visiting a mirror shop."

"Sure," Maddix had replied, without thinking it all through. "But, just asking, why a mirror shop?"

"Because you'll have plenty of time to poke around." When he had seen Maddix's confused expression, he had explained, "The shop's old and closed down years ago. I happened to know the old owner and he said we could use all the abandoned mirrors there."

"Okay," Maddix had nodded. "When is it?"

"Tomorrow, actually," Mr. Vincent had answered. "At noon."

Maddix thought about another time earlier that day.

He had been running to catch up with Luke, who had raced him to the Dining Hall. But, he was stopped by Dagner. He called, "Parker!" Wondering why he always called him by his last name, Maddix doubled back.

"Did Mr. Vincent tell you about the field trip?"

"Yes," Maddix said.

"Just making sure," he said. As Maddix walked away, Dagner said, "And, I think you'll find the mirrors very interesting. People tend to get *sucked in.*"

Sucked in... what on earth had he been talking about?

As Maddix sat in his room, his stomach turned over; Mythology was *Dagner's class.* How could he have been so stupid to accept? *Actually,* he thought, *I wouldn't have declined it even if I knew it was Dagner's class. Nicole's my friend, and if Dagner did something to her...*

Maddix pondered Dagner's words. As he stared out the window, he noticed that the moon had arrived early. Or had it? If that white shape in the distance wasn't the moon, what was it?

Suddenly, there was a blinding light. There was a soft hiss, and a slam. A voice—a cold voice—whispered, "*Mirrors.*"

Maddix sat up in his bed. What had happened? Had he been dreaming? *No,* he thought, *it seemed so real.*

He got up and searched for the white shape, but it had disappeared. *Mirrors*—wasn't that what the field trip was about? Wasn't he going to visit a mirror shop? He didn't know how he knew it, but danger was coming, and it was coming fast.

"Wake up!" someone was shouting. Luke was shaking him awake.

"What is it?" Maddix asked him.

"It's almost noon!" Luke exclaimed. "Why'd you sleep in?"

"I didn't—sleep in? What?" Maddix said.

"Come on!" Luke urged. He left.

A moment later, Maddix, dressed and bewildered as ever, rushed down the hallway.

"There you are!" Luke said.

"I want answers," Maddix told him. "Why'd I sleep in?"

"How would I know?" Luke asked. "It's your brain that slept more than it usually does!"

Suddenly, Mr. Vincent rounded the corner.

"Boys," he said, "it's time for the field trip."

Luke and Maddix followed him to the school grounds. A bus was there, students filing into it. But there was something weird about the bus—it had wings! Maddix gasped. Sure, he was a bit behind magic-wise, but *anyone* would've been amazed if they saw a bus with wings!

He spotted Nicole, her face anxious. She was looking around. Maddix and Luke hurried over to her.

"Where were you?" she asked, angry that they were late (but also very relieved that they came at all). "I've been waiting!"

"Sorry," Maddix said. "I overslept."

"You? Oversleeping?" Nicole said. "I haven't known you a very long time, but I know you aren't the kind of person who sleeps in." Maddix laughed and followed his friends onto a bus marked seven.

In a low voice, Maddix told Luke and Nicole about the mysterious voice the previous night.

"Mirrors?" Nicole repeated. "What do you think that means?"

"Maybe there's gonna be danger in the mirror shop," Maddix said.

"Is someone out to get you?" Luke asked.

Maddix shrugged. "Dagner is all I can think of when you say that. Remember: 'You're not *telling* Parker about this, are you?'"

"Yeah, I was gonna ask you guys about that," Nicole said. "I did some researching, and found out that, back in 1981, enchanters—yes, enchant*ers*, not enchantresses— always followed those whom they disliked. They were always sneaking around behind them, plotting evil plans."

"You could recite the whole passage of where you read that, couldn't you?" Luke said.

"Yup," Nicole said brightly. "*The methods in 1981 are still standing today. Enchanters in that year began following their enemies. You might think of it as prowling for prey. This method was introduced by Leonard Scottner, a man with no thought for the consequences of his actions. He had a grudge against a certain Bill Hemmings, and Scottner stalked him in all his years at school. (Where he went to school exactly is unknown, though recent discoveries show that he may have attended Apollo Academy before it closed down.) Scottner kept an eye on Hemmings for so long, Hemmings had noticed that he was being followed. Eventually, Hemmings caught on to Scottner and his plans, leaving Scottner in a very uncomfortable position.*"

Luke and Maddix just stared at her.

"What?" Nicole said. "My dad did a good job in keeping me interested in research."

"Wait—Nicole," Maddix said, "you said that Hemmings caught on to his plans."

"Yeah," Nicole replied. "So?"

"It's not that surprising," Luke said. "I mean, someone *has* to notice if someone's watching their every move."

"The author—" Maddix began.

"Carl Brickens," Nicole said.

"Right," Maddix nodded. "Brickens said that he— Scottner—was left in an uncomfortable position. What did he mean?"

"Nicole," Luke said, turning to her, "did the book—"

"*Great Explanations*," Nicole said.

"Did *Great Explanations* say anything after what you said to us?"

"No," Nicole shook her head. "The next chapter came after that."

"A weird place to end a chapter," Maddix said.

The bus had been flying over the country, looking down on hills and trees and farms. Now they were overlooking a town, its residents not noticing a flying bus. Maddix wondered if it was invisible.

"Usually, Flying Buses are faster," Nicole said, looking out the window. "But I guess the budget's too low to get faster ones."

"What do you mean?" Luke asked. "The budget at Apollo is great!"

"Not recently," Nicole shook her head. She gave Luke her pity look again. "Don't you know? Because some kid slipped and fell in the Dining Hall, their parents sued the school."

"Sued us?" Luke exploded. "*Sued us?* They can *do* that?"

Nicole nodded. "Yes."

"That's just dumb," Maddix said.

"But I think it's fair," Nicole said. "I mean, there's no law that says who can sue who."

"You scare me, you know that?" Luke said. He looked at Maddix, who shrugged.

"Yes, we're here!" he exclaimed. Luke pointed to a shabby, run-down building as the bus descended. There was a sign hanging on its side, saying MIRRORS: THE FINE ART OF REFLECTION. Another sign was plastered over the door: CLOSED: FOREVER!

"Huh," Maddix said, pointing to this, "not many people would say something was closed forever."

"I know," Luke said. "It *could* open again. Some places that people think are closed for good open up again. I mean, look at Apollo! We were closed for years and opened again!"

"You're right," Nicole said. (Maddix thought that this was something she would rarely say to Luke). "I read a book that had a list of all the buildings in the United States that were closed for the longest time and most likely to never be opened again."

"Umm... that's random," Maddix said, "any other obscure facts you'd like to share?"

Nicole shrugged. "But can you guess what number Apollo was?"

"What?" Luke and Maddix asked.

"Number three," Nicole said. "Number two was an old warehouse in Colorado, and number one was this mirror shop."

"Wow," Maddix said. "In all of the United States, Apollo was the third most likely to never open again. And it opened!"

"And the mirror shop we're going into right now is number one," Luke said darkly. "I bet you anything it's haunted."

"Haunted?" Nicole repeated. "My dad told me that nothing's haunted."

"Sure," Luke said. "Sure, keep telling yourself that."

They got out of the bus and went into the mirror shop with the rest of Nicole's class. An old man was standing behind a counter, smirking at them. Maddix stepped back. Luke pushed him forward.

"Don't be scared, Maddix," he said. "It's fine." But it *wasn't* fine to Maddix; there was something about that man that made Maddix feel a sharp pain in his arm when he looked at him.

"Gather round, everyone," said Dagner, standing in front of the class. "Welcome to the The Fine Art of Reflection. In other words, a mirror shop. I would like you to meet Wilfred Ridson." He indicated the man, who waved (Maddix felt another pain in his arm). "He will tell you a little bit about the mirrors here and then we can look around."

"Thank you, Lucian," said Wilfred Ridson. "Now, children, these mirrors are ancient—as you can probably tell. Most of them are just over five hundred years old. As you might have noticed, I said most of them, not all of them. For there is one mirror—the oldest mirror in history—that is over one million years old. I have been asked if that is an exaggeration, merely a customer-intriguer, but think: I haven't had customers in over one hundred years! I call the million-year-old mirror the Tall-Tale Mirror, or the TTM, because people think I am saying tall tales. The TTM is placed in this very shop—right in its heart. Find it, and you will surely find its secret."

Though Maddix felt pain whenever he looked at this man, he couldn't help liking his style. He made Maddix want to find the TTM.

"Thank you," Ridson was saying. "And now you can explore the shop—and see what wonders are in store!"

"Weird man, isn't he?" Luke said.

"Yeah," Maddix said.

"Do you want to look for the TTM?" Nicole asked.

"Definitely," Luke said. "There's something about Ridson—he made me want to find it."

"I know," Maddix said. "I like the way he talks. Very calm, yet enthusiastic."

"And impressive," Luke added.

Maddix nodded.

"Hey," Luke said to him. "Earlier, when you stepped back from him? What was that about? Were you scared or something?"

"No," Maddix shook his head. "It's just—whenever I look at him, my arm hurts. It's like I know him or something."

"Hmmm," Nicole said. "I feel like I read about Recognition Pains *somewhere...*"

"Recognition Pains," Luke repeated. "Hmm, sounds strange. Are you sure they exist?"

"Yes," Nicole said. "I'm sure my dad told me *something...*"

They started walking around the shop. Luke pointed at a mirror that looked particularly aged.

"How old do you think it is?" he asked.

Maddix shrugged. "Eighty?"

"Eighty?" Nicole said. "No, it's looks more like one hundred."

"You guys can't be serious," Luke said. "Ridson said that most of these mirrors are over *five hundred* years old, and all you can think of is one hundred?"

"You're right, you're right," Maddix said. "How about four hundred ninety-nine?"

Luke laughed. "Very funny. Let's check out some other mirrors." They passed a lot of other mirrors and reached a fork. Nicole looked back.

"Um, guys... where is everyone?"

"I don't know," Luke replied. "We're probably just really deep into the shop or something. Anyway, this is getting boring. We should split up so we can go faster, and maybe one of us would find the TTM. Maddix, you go right, Nicole, you go left, and I'll go straight." They did as they were told.

Maddix was far into the walls of mirrors when he heard a scuffling noise. He whipped around: nothing. He walked on.

Later, he heard a whispering. He couldn't make out the words, but he knew they were saying *something*.

Maddix looked around nervously, shrugged, and kept looking for the TTM. A few moments later, someone grabbed him by the mouth and forced him backward into a shadowy corner.

"Hey!"

A tall figure stood before him, with sleek black hair and smile: it was Lucian Dagner.

"Sorry, did I frighten you?" he asked politely.

Yeah! Maddix wanted to say back. *How would you like it if someone grabbed you by the mouth and pushed you away?*

"Yeah, a little bit," he said.

"Again, my apologies," he sounded nicer than usual. "I just wanted to know whether you'd found the TTM yet."

"Oh, no," Maddix said. "I was just looking for it, though. With Luke and Nicole."

"But where are they now?" Dagner asked, looking around.

"We split up," Maddix said, wondering why he was telling him this, "Luke thought our chances of finding the TTM were better if we'd look apart."

"Very wise choice," Dagner said. "May I help you look?"

"Sure, I guess," Maddix said, without thinking. Afterward, he thought, *Ah, darn it! Why'd I say that? Only a stupid person would let a man like Dagner look for a mysterious mirror with them!* But, if he'd said no, what would be an excuse? So he shouldn't *totally* beat himself up for his choice.

After a long, silent search of mirrors, Dagner stopped Maddix by holding out his arm.

"Stop."

"What is it?" Maddix asked.

"This is it," Dagner said softly. "The Tall-Tale Mirror." He pointed a shaking finger at an extremely dusty mirror. It was tall and important-looking, though very shabby and old all the same.

"It looks a bit weary, doesn't it?" Dagner asked.

"I suppose so," Maddix shrugged. At the same time, he and Dagner walked up to it. Suddenly, Dagner became his creepy self again as he spoke.

"What is within this mirror?" he asked. Maddix looked at him; who was talking to? Maddix guessed he was talking to him, so he said, "Within it? How could something be within it?"

"Yes, something is always within a mirror. If you lean in closely, then you can see a bit of what is within it."

"Really?" Maddix asked suspiciously.

"Step forward," Dagner said.

Maddix knew about characters in movies that listened to the bad guys blindly and ended up in a really bad position... like dead. So, he said, "I'll only step forward if *you* step forward."

"Okay," Dagner said, looking at him strangely.

"One, two, three," Maddix and Dagner stepped closer to the mirror. Maddix looked at himself, wondering if this was a trick. Or...

What if there *was* something within the mirror? Did it have secrets that it hadn't revealed? Was there something about its age that was special to it?

Maddix looked at himself a little more, and looked at Dagner. He was staring at Maddix fixedly.

"What are you doing?" Maddix asked.

"Nothing," Dagner said. Maddix looked uncertainly at him.

Suddenly, Dagner pushed him into the glass, and Maddix was swallowed by darkness.

CHAPTER 12
THE VISION

S idero, if I may—"

"*Don't touch me!*"

"But sir—"

"Don't!"

Sidero was in pain. He clutched his chest, falling on the ground. As he fell, the floor shook. Zennith didn't expect it not to; the old and abandoned shack was extremely broken-down.

"Sidero, let me just ask what happened."

"Well, Zennith," Sidero said, trying to pick himself up but failing and falling back down with a crash, "I-I had a vision."

"A vision, sir?" Zennith asked tentatively.

"About—about the boy," Sidero said, still gripping his chest.

"What about him? What was he doing?" Zennith asked, offering a hand.

"He—he was falling," Sidero replied, pushing his hand away. "There was darkness around him—I think it was Lucian's doing."

"Dagner's, sir?" Zennith's brow was furrowed.

"Yes," Sidero nodded. He closed his eyes. "Yes, it was definitely the work of Lucian."

"Should we send him another message, sir?" Zennith asked.

"About what?" Sidero opened his eyes. "We only send messages if the concept is very detailed and should be answered in equal detail. We can use the barrel."

"The barrel, sire?"

"Bring it to me."

Zennith put a hand in his pocket and withdrew a very small piece of wood. Sidero closed his eyes again and focused on the wood and it rose up into the air. There was a small pop! and it started to grow bigger and bigger, until it was a barrel. Zennith stared at it as it filled up with water. Except, this wasn't normal water. It was Communication Water.

"Lucian Dagner!" Sidero shouted, and the water sparkled and made popping noises. Suddenly, the face of Lucian Dagner appeared in the water.

"You called?"

"Lucian," Sidero said, "what did you do to the Parker boy?"

"Simple question, simple answer, Sidero," Dagner said sardonically, "I used the classic 'keep an eye on the victim and throw him into an old mirror' trick."

"You chucked him into a mirror?" Zennith asked.

"Yes," Dagner nodded. "But it wasn't that easy. The boy was suspicious."

"You mean he knew of your intentions?" Zennith said.

"Not entirely," Dagner responded. "I saw the look on his face; he was hesitant when I asked him to step closer to the mirror—so I could push him, of course—and he seemed to know what was going on. I listened to him, Mr. Vincent's son, and that Rader girl talk about my methods."

"They know too much!" Sidero exclaimed.

"Calm down, sir," Dagner said. "I have it all under control."

"Lucian, where is the boy at the moment?" Zennith asked. "Sidero had a vision; Parker was falling in darkness."

"Ah, yes," Dagner nodded and smirked. "Yes, yes, that is exactly where he should be."

"But where is he?" Zennith said. "Where is he falling to?"

"Somewhere in which I have great connections," Dagner's smirk became more pronounced. "They will be able to hold him at bay long enough for me to commence stage four."

"Who's 'they?'" Zennith asked. "And what is stage four?"

"All questions will be answered," Dagner said, "or be figured out. Trust me to know what I'm doing."

"Our expectations our high, Lucian," Sidero told his servant. "Don't let us down."

"I won't," Dagner replied. And, with that, he vanished. Sidero changed the barrel into a small piece of wood again and Zennith placed it back into his pocket, a look of disbelief on his face.

"But will he, sire?"

"What do you mean?" Sidero asked. "Can you possibly be afraid that his plan is too dangerous? Can you possibly be feeling scared for the boy?"

"Of course not!" Zennith stepped back, offended. But, all the same, as Sidero's back was turned, Zennith muttered, "Man, that kid better hope he's got backup."

CHAPTER 13
THUNDERBIRDS

Everyone says it's okay to be frustrated sometimes, but not everyone has been falling down forever!" Maddix's words came out icy and mean. "Sorry," he said, to no one in particular. "Bit weird, falling in darkness, though." He felt that someone was there. He groped around in the air as he fell, thinking that he would at least pass time by doing something—even if that something was feeling around for another falling thing or person he didn't even know existed. Maddix just got this feeling that someone was right next to him—but was there?

"Hello?" he said uncertainly. "Is anyone there? Ah!" He had heard a scuffling noise.

"Mirrors... mirrors..."

Maddix recognized the whisper—the one that had spoken to him before the field trip! Following it had been a lot of light—Maddix covered his eyes, thinking it would come again. But it didn't, so Maddix took his hands from his eyes and looked around.

"S-show yourself!" he stammered. He didn't like it that he was showing cowardice and how scared he was in front of something evil.

"*I told you about the mirrors,*" the voice said, "*but some people never listen, do they?*"

"Who are you?" Maddix asked.

"*I think you know who I am,*" the voice said. "*You have fought one of my servants—*"

"And won!" Maddix interrupted, spinning foolishly on the spot, trying to find the source of the voice.

"*Sheer luck,*" the voice snarled. "*Only by sheer luck could you have won against one of MY servants.*"

"Are—are you Sidero?" Maddix asked, his worst fears confirmed.

"*What do you think?*" the voice said. It became *very* annoying.

"You're Sidero!" Maddix exclaimed.

"*Not exactly,*" the voice said. "*I am your worst nightmare.*"

"Come again?" Maddix said, leaning in.

"*I am the disembodied voice and spirit of Sidero,*" he said.

"Okay then. Close enough," Maddix said.

"*Aren't you scared?*" Sidero asked.

"Yeah, totally," Maddix said sarcastically, "and now I'm going to sprout wings and fly."

"*Har, har,*" Sidero said. "*You might sneer now, Parker, but mark my words: you won't be sneering when I'm done with you.*"

"What do you mean?" Maddix said, fear coming back into his voice.

"*You'll see,*" Sidero said.

Maddix wanted to question him further, but there was a small *pop!* and there was no sound. Sidero must've left.

However, Maddix had bigger things to worry about: where was he falling to?

Suddenly, something poked him in the back. He whipped around, looking for what did. Then, something poked him in the neck. He turned back around and saw nothing.

There was a cackling and something grabbed him by the arms as he was falling, leaving him suspended in midair. Though very scary, it was kind of a relief; Maddix had been growing tired of falling.

"Let me go!" Maddix shouted.

"Never!" cried a voice. It sounded insane; it was one of those voices that you'd think the person (or thing) whose voice it was had laughed a little too much.

There was a swooshing noise, and Maddix was going up, up, up...

He turned a corner. Where were they taking him?

"I don't know who you are, but put me down this instant!" Maddix said forcefully.

"Our master has requested us to do this," said another voice, lower and deeper than normal. "So if you have any objections—and I know you do—tell them to him."

"Who? Sidero's servant?" Maddix said, without thinking. One of the beings was so surprised that they almost dropped him.

"You *dare* speak his name?"

"Yeah, I dare," Maddix said, feeling he had some power over them now, "and if you don't let me go, I'll keep saying his name over and over again."

"Nice try," the second being said, "but we've got orders."

"Yeah," said the first. "Taunt us all you like, but we've never failed to carry out orders from our master—especially this one."

"Well, I need to know what kind of thing these faithful followers of Sidero are," Maddix said, imagining winged monkeys from *The Wizard of Oz*.

"We are Thunderbirds," the first said proudly. "My name's Cacklefront, and this is Fielderlow."

"Interesting," Maddix said. "So, I'm wondering—how does it feel to serve the most powerful enchanter in the world?"

"He only chooses the best to serve him," said Cacklefront, and Maddix imagined him throwing out his chest indignantly. "His servant knew he could count on me and Fielderlow to take care of 'certain trouble.'"

"Certain trouble, you say?" Maddix repeated. "What did he mean?"

"Course, he meant you," Cacklefront replied. "Who else? Big deal, you are."

"I am?" Maddix asked. "What are you talking about?"

"My master, he's got a problem with you," Cacklefront said seriously. "But he won't say much of what it is, he's a secretive guy—"

"That's enough, Cacklefront," Fielderlow said sternly.

"But I was just—"

He was cut off by Fielderlow repeating, "Enough!"

"Could we talk about this?" Cacklefront asked.

"No," Fielderlow said firmly. "We talked about it before, there is no reason to talk about it now—"

"Excuse me, Mr. Fielderlow, sir?" Maddix asked nervously, trying to be polite to the superior Thunderbird to get him to do what he wanted. "Er— could you consider Cacklefront's request?"

"What do you mean, kid? You're our prisoner!" Fielderlow's voice became less solemn and more mad.

"I mean," Maddix said calmly, "that you could talk about the situation before *certain people* get annoying."

"You mean yourself?" Cacklefront said.

"No, I mean you," Maddix said. "If anyone knows about annoying people, it's me."

"Alright," Fielderlow said after a short pause. "Cacklefront, let's go to the next landing."

Landing... so they were somewhere with landings, Maddix thought, *interesting.*

The two Thunderbirds landed on a hard surface and dropped Maddix onto it.

"If you move," Fielderlow said to him, "there will be pain."

"Okay," Maddix lied.

Fielderlow turned to Cacklefront. "What is it?"

"Master says that we should be communicating more," Cacklefront said.

"To each other, not to prisoners!" Fielderlow replied. "Cacklefront, what would happen if he escaped and told our master's secrets to the whole world?"

"That's not gonna happen." Maddix pictured Cacklefront waving a hand. "He's not gonna escape as long as we keep an eye on him."

"Well, right now, we're not keeping an eye on him!" Fielderlow exclaimed, "He could just crawl away any second, this landing's the biggest one in the chute—"

"Ha!" Cacklefront pointed at him. "Look who's giving away information now!"

"I—well, the point is," Fielderlow said, "if he escapes, it's our fault, because he's our responsibility. Do you want our master to rely on us to do dangerous missions like this again? He's not going to be happy if this boy disappears."

Maddix started to crawl away silently, feeling around as he went. He stopped when Cacklefront asked, "But what's so special about him, anyway? Master says he's different, but how? He seems normal to me."

"He's covering up his powers," Fielderlow responded. "He's hiding them—and I'm afraid to say that he's doing a good job."

Powers, Maddix thought suddenly, *that's right—my powers! I could use them to get out of here!*

He turned back.

"Thunderbirds, sirs?" Maddix asked uncertainly.

"What?" they both said.

"I need to see how big and powerful you are," he said. "I've never seen a Thunderbird, you know."

"Oh, you've got to see my wings," Cacklefront said gleefully, "and my eyes—people say they could kill. I don't know if that's really true, though…"

"Really, Cacklefront, is this the time?" Fielderlow asked.

"Yes it is!" Cacklefront replied. "He might not live to see a Thunderbird!"

Maddix's stomach turned over; he might not live? What were they talking about? Were they going to bring him to Sidero himself?

"Light a candle," Fielderlow said resentfully. He added sharply, "*Quickly.*"

"Yes!" Cacklefront exclaimed. Maddix envisioned he'd pulled out a candle and lit it delightedly.

There was a flicker of light as the candle lit up. Maddix gasped as he saw a hawk-like face, lined and gaunt-looking. The wings were a sapphire blue, and the eyes were beady and yellow. Fielderlow wasn't much different: his wings were more of a navy blue, his eyes were more narrower than Cacklefront's, and his face was more a falcon's then a hawk's.

"Whoa," Maddix said, stepping back. Cacklefront was in his element.

"I know, right? People say that my wings could make a more powerful storm than his. Tornadoes and hurricanes are cool, sure, but what about earthquakes and tsunamis? I also like to intimidate people with my looks, see if they cower. Sometimes, people cower so much that I can just walk right around them—they don't even put up a fight! Oh, and—"

"Enough, Cacklefront," said Fielderlow, and Cacklefront fell silent. Fielderlow turned to Maddix, "Well, now that you've seen us, what are you gonna do now?"

"This," Maddix said, and he fixed his eyes on Fielderlow's, focusing every particle of his body on entering his mind. He closed his eyes and saw the familiar dancing flames. He made the DWAH face, and he saw flames.

Then, letters and numbers appeared around him, flying everywhere. Maddix searched for a way to stop him—any thought, feeling, look—*there!*

Far away, there was a thought that read: *Don't let the kid near the light; it can control Thunderbirds! Cacklefront, don't you KNOW that?*

So all Maddix had to do was take the candle Cacklefront had taken out and place the fire on Fielderlow and Cacklefront, and he could escape! But how could he go up, to where Nicole and Luke were? And Dagner—he would get into *so* much trouble!

Maddix tried to think quickly, knowing he had only seconds before he would go back to the present. Then it hit him—not an idea, but something actually hit him. Make that *shocked* him. Something was glowing in his pocket. He pulled out—a pencil. *What's this pencil doing here?* He wondered. *And why is it glowing like that? Did it shock me?* He read something on it: *Electro Pencil. What's an Electro Pencil?* He thought. Then, as if answering his question, writing appeared right next to the eraser.

M-Point the tip at the ceiling. It'll help you out. More info later. Don't tell anyone. -S

Maddix stared at it, unblinking. *Why would I point it at the ceiling?* He wondered. *And who's S? Why can't I tell anyone?* But he knew he was running out of time; he would go back to the Thunderbirds soon.

Maddix took a breath, and decided to take the Electro Pencil's word. A second later, the words faded away.

Maddix didn't have time to wonder what happened: in a whirl of color, he was back with Fielderlow and Cacklefront, both looking at him like he was crazy.

"Kid?" Cacklefront said. "Are you okay?"

"Oh no," Fielderlow whispered, "he's making the DWAH face—quick, Cacklefront, close your mind!"

"How am I supposed to do that?" he asked.

"Too late, boys," Maddix said, waving the Electro Pencil.

"Look, it's an Electro Pencil!" Cacklefront pointed excitedly at it. "Don't you see it, Fielderlow? Those are really rare—how'd you get a hold one one?"

"Doesn't matter," Maddix said, his voice strong. "Time is up—at least for you two." He yanked his hand into the air, the Electro Pencil held high. Electric beams shot out of the tip, and metal came crashing down.

"The chute!" Fielderlow shouted over the din. "It's collapsing!"

"I can see that!" Cacklefront yelled. "Let's get out of here!"

"What about the prisoner?" Fielderlow asked.

"Forget him!" Cacklefront bellowed. "Save yourself while you can!" They flew up, up, up...and they were gone. Maddix had the urge to grab one of the large falling fragments, so he did. He hopped onto it, and to his amazement, it floated upward. The fragment was emitting gas, and it created enough force to carry both itself and Maddix to the top of the chute.

A few moments later, Maddix saw a flash of light— the mirror! He cried, "Stop!" And miraculously, the fragment came to a halt. He was close enough to push the glass and step back into the mirror shop. Someone was running to him, arms outstretched.

"Maddix!"

CHAPTER 14
SUSPICIONS

W hen I ask you this question, Sidero, answer me with complete honesty," Zennith said, looking seriously at his master. "I need you to tell me if you think Lucian's plan is too dangerous."

"Too dangerous?" Sidero repeated. "Zennith, as long as the boy gets here in one piece, I don't care how dangerous it is."

"But… but what if something—happened?" Zennith couldn't find the right words to say. He didn't want to act soft, but he was a bit worried. What if Dagner did something to the boy? What if he hurt him way too much? What if—?

"What?" Sidero walked towards him. "What could you possibly think is just a little too dangerous for your liking?"

"Not just mine, but ours," Zennith didn't give him a straight answer. "Would *you* feel uncomfortable if—?"

"If *what*, Zennith?" Sidero glared at him. "What? Answer me!"

Zennith hesitated. "What if he—I don't know—killed him?"

"Killed him?" Sidero laughed so hard he wheezed. "*Killed him?* Zennith, no one's going to kill him!"

"Really?" Zennith stepped backward. "No one's going to kill him?"

"Of course not!" Sidero exclaimed. "Who am I, Lord Voldemort? I'm not going to make that mistake."

"What are you going to do to him, then?" Zennith asked hesitantly.

"I'll tell you soon," Sidero said. "I have big plans for him."

"You're scaring me," Zennith said. "Big plans? What do you mean?"

"All questions will be answered in due time," Sidero said. Then, his expression softened. "But, don't worry, I'm not going to kill him."

"Good," Zennith sighed. Sidero looked at him, his eyes saying, *Are you feeling the need to protect him?* "I mean," he said quickly, "it's good you're not going *too* severe—at least just yet."

"Right," Sidero smiled. Zennith walked away, and he muttered, "Not just yet."

Later, Sidero paced around in his hiding place.

"*What* is going on with Zennith?" he said feverishly. "I'm losing my servant, this boy is getting to me, and I'm falling apart! What is happening to me? Parker has got something I don't, I need to see what he's up to... I also need to see what Lucian's doing with him... how can I do both? Ah..." He sent a letter to Zennith.

Zennith—
I need you to make a nighttime visit to Parker tomorrow.

That night, Zennith met up with Sidero on another hill.

"You know about the last time I made a night visit to him, don't you?" he asked.

"I am aware," Sidero replied, "but I need you to try again. Except, this time, Parker won't know it's you. I need you to go in disguise."

"As what?" Zennith asked uncertainly. He would do a lot of things for Sidero, but he was very sensitive about what he wore.

"Just dress in black," Sidero told him. "Be as black as the night, as stealthy as a ninja, and as quick as a flash of light."

"Got it," Zennith responded. "Tonight, midnight."

"I can always count on you," Sidero said.

"Yes, you can," Zennith agreed.

CHAPTER 15
THE DARK OF THE NIGHT

Nicole threw her arms around him.

"Maddix, we were so worried!" she exclaimed. Luke's face was white.

"What happened?" he asked. "We haven't seen you in hours, so we met up and checked some video cameras. We saw Dagner pushing you into the mirror. How'd you get out?"

"I'll tell you later," Maddix said, as he heard footsteps.

"Hello, there!" Ridson made his way towards them. "Seems there's been a bit of trouble with a mirror. Is this it?"

"Yes," Maddix replied. "And this is the TTM."

"Is that so?" Ridson's eyes widened. "Why, yes it is! Good job!"

"Mr. Ridson, sir?" Nicole asked. "Do you know if there's anything—er—special about it? Secret powers? Strange enchantments?"

"I told you there's a secret about it," Ridson said. "Do you know what it is?"

"No, sir," Maddix said quickly. "We've looked for hours, but we can't find it. Can you show us some other mirrors?"

"Afraid I can't," Ridson checked his watch. "It's time for you to get back onto your bus. Where is Mr. Dagner?"

Where *was* Dagner? Maddix expected him to be there, right beside the mirror, admiring how great his plan worked. But he was nowhere in sight.

"Maybe he's near the front." No sooner had Luke said it than Lucian Dagner himself strolled around the corner and approached him. His eyes found Maddix, and Maddix thought he saw a flicker of surprise on Dagner's face. But, he couldn't check, because Dagner had turned to Ridson.

"Wilfred, I think it's time to go back to Apollo Academy," he said.

"Yes, that's just what I was telling these children," Ridson responded. Maddix, without thinking, made the DWAH face, saw fire, and entered Dagner's mind.

A thought, right near the front, was displayed. It said: *Children indeed, Ridson, but you don't know what they're capable of. What on Earth is Parker doing here? Cacklefront and Fielderlow have failed—wait till I tell Sidero...*

Then, Maddix was back in front of the TTM, staring hard at Dagner.

"Maddix?" Luke was waving his hand in front of his face. "Maddix..."

"What—yeah?" Maddix jerked back to life.

"What're you doing?" Luke asked. Nicole nudged him.

"Yes, what *were* you doing, Parker?" Dagner sneered.

"Nothing," Maddix said quickly.

They got on the bus, Maddix's eyes on Dagner, who was sitting near the front.

When they arrived back at Apollo Academy, Maddix, Luke, and Nicole ran to Maddix and Luke's bedroom. Nicole closed the curtains and flipped on the lights.

"So," Luke said, sitting on Maddix's bed, "what happened in the mirror?"

Maddix explained about Sidero's voice and his encounter with the Thunderbirds, Cacklefront and Fielderlow. Next, he told them about how he'd used his powers to enter Fielderlow's mind and find key information. And he told them about the Electro Pencil, pulling it out of his pocket (they gawked at it in awe). Then, he filled them in on how he'd entered Dagner's mind and looked at what he was thinking.

"And then, I found out that he was surprised to see me—of course—and that he knew Cacklefront and Fielderlow had failed and was going to tell Sidero. He also was thinking that we were capable of lots of things. It was really creepy."

"So Dagner's impressed?" Luke asked.

"I think so," Maddix replied. "He's definitely shocked that I'm alive."

"Alive?" Nicole repeated. "Maddix, what do you mean, 'alive?'"

"He probably wants to bring him to Sidero, who wants him dead or something," Luke said casually.

"Come on," Nicole said, "someone like Sidero's not *that* stupid. He knows not to make such silly mistakes. And, you'll totally see it coming. You already know so much—too much, in Sidero's opinion."

Before Luke or Maddix could say anything in response, there was a knock on the door and someone came in: That someone was Mr. Vincent.

"Hello," he said.

"Hi, Dad," Luke said.

"What're you up to?" Mr. Vincent asked.

"Nothing," Nicole replied. "We're... um... talking."

"Talking?" Mr. Vincent raised his eyebrows. "About what?"

"Normal stuff," Maddix shrugged.

"Like a certain mirror?"

Maddix stared at him. They had all agreed *not* to tell Mr. Vincent, since he might not believe him. *Well, this proved us wrong, I guess*, Maddix thought.

"Excuse me?" he said.

"Are you three talking about the Tall-Tale Mirror?" Mr. Vincent asked.

"I guess you could say that," Nicole said slowly.

"Okay," Mr. Vincent said.

"Okay," Luke said. Mr. Vincent left.

Cold night air filled Maddix and Luke's bedroom as Maddix himself stared at the ceiling. *Did Mr. Vincent know about the TTM?* Maddix wondered. *Did he know that I'd gone into it? But news couldn't've traveled that fast. Okay, Ridson knew about it, but only part of it. But this didn't make sense…*

Lost in thought, Maddix closed his eyes and fell asleep.

Around midnight, the floorboards creaked. Zennith crept along the hallway, scanning the door numbers. He found Maddix's and slipped into the room. Closing the door carefully behind him, Zennith made his way towards Maddix's bed. He hit Maddix's forehead gently with his finger as he stirred. Zennith took out a small computer chip from his pocket and placed it in Maddix's right ear. He tapped on his watch and whispered, "Phase one, complete."

He left the room, and sneaked into Dagner's room a few hallways away.

"Lucian!" he whispered. "Lucian!"

Dagner woke up, saw Zennith, and asked, "Has phase one commenced?"

"Yes, I've just told Sidero so," Zennith answered.

"Good," Dagner got out of bed, put his coat on, and walked to the courtyard. He tapped on his watch and took out a controller from his coat pocket. He connected his watch to the controller, so he could operate the controller from his watch. Dagner twisted a dial and turned on the device in Maddix's ear.

"Phase two, complete." He said.

He made his way back into the school, feeling very evil—as he should.

CHAPTER 16
~~DAGNER~~ DANGER

R eally, Luke, I think that's a step too far," Nicole
protested to Luke's let's-go-spy-on-Dagner idea.
"Come on, he's spying on us right now!"
Luke exclaimed. He turned to Maddix. "What do you
think?"

"I don't know," Maddix shrugged. "I guess Nicole's
right. Give him a chance."

"Give the guy who pushed you into a mirror a
chance?" Luke said, bewildered. "I thought you'd be on
my side! It's just lucky you got stuck with the dumb
Thunderbirds! If they had more than half a brain, they
would've killed you."

"Killed him?" Nicole repeated. "I don't think that's
what they'd do. The worst they could do to him is take
him to Sidero."

"That's pretty bad!" Luke exclaimed. Maddix was busy scratching his right ear. It was itching like mad.

"What's up with this thing?" he asked.

"What thing?" Luke and Nicole replied together.

"My ear," Maddix responded. "It's killing me."

"Let me see," Nicole checked inside his ear. "I don't see anythi—whoa."

"What is it?" Maddix asked.

"There's something in your ear," Nicole whispered. When she spoke, she blew in his ear.

"Stop talking, you're making me get chills," Maddix told her.

"Sorry," she said, "it's just—what is that?"

"What is what?" Luke asked her.

"There's a black thing," Nicole said.

"A what?" Luke said, stepping over to her and trying to see.

"No," Nicole replied, "it looks like a chip..."

"A chip?" Luke repeated. "Let me see that." He gasped.

"What are you guys seeing?" Maddix tried to turn around, but Nicole shouted, "Don't move! I'm gonna take it out."

"*What?*"

Nicole extracted a black chip from Maddix's ear.

"What is this?" she asked.

"How would I know?" Maddix said.

"It was in *your* ear," Nicole said.

"Well I don't know what it is," Maddix told her. They turned to Luke, who shrugged.

Nicole took the chip to her bedroom and tried to figure out what it was used for. She had no luck.

Days went by, and Maddix and Luke became paranoid about Dagner; he seemed to be everywhere they were. Was he following them? Maddix was reminded of the conversation Dagner had had with Luke's father. He *was* following them! As the days turned into weeks, Maddix and Luke longed for another adventure.

"Let's do something fun," Luke said one day. "You know, daring. Nicole shouldn't be involved—she's got that chip on her mind day and night."

"I guess we could," Maddix said, "and don't blame Nicole, thank her. We would have never gotten this far if it wasn't for her."

"I guess," Luke shrugged. "So, what should we do?"

They sat and thought. Suddenly, Luke sat up. "What if it involved Dagner?"

"I don't know, Luke," Maddix said. "We could get into serious trouble."

"It's fine," Luke told him. "And it's just a harmless little joke, he's never gonna catch us."

"Alright," Maddix said. "What's your idea?"

"Here's the plan," Luke whispered his plan to Maddix, who nodded.

The next day was the perfect day of the week to play a joke on a teacher: Friday. Dagner, if he *did* catch them (which they hoped wouldn't happen), would have to search all over the building for them because it was the weekend, and nobody went anywhere near a learning place on the weekend.

Maddix and Luke asked Mr. Vincent what lessons they'd be taking notes on today. He said that they had Mythology at three o'clock—right near the end of the day. Everything was perfect—the time of the lesson, the day of the week, everything.

Maddix and Luke made their way to Ancient Artifacts class, chatting about how good the day was turning out to be already.

All the lessons went by really fast, and so did lunch. Before they knew it, Maddix and Luke were heading to Dagner's classroom. Maddix was nervous; what if they were caught? What would happen then? Teachers punished the students by having them clean the parts of the school that people stayed away from. But would Dagner do that to Maddix and Luke? Or worse—would he think Nicole was part of it, and punish her too? What if she got expelled? *You're over-thinking this,* he told himself, *just be calm and play it cool. If you pull this off, you'll be alright. If you don't—we'll cross that bridge when we get to it.*

Maddix and Luke entered the classroom, trying not to look too guilty—even if they hadn't done anything yet.

Dagner had made the room smell musty and the walls looked like they hadn't been cleaned in twenty years. Typical. The one thing that caught Maddix's eye was the book on Dagner's desk. It was entitled: *Sneak Attacks: How to Master the Element of Surprise.* Why would he leave it for everyone to see? Obviously, he was evil, but putting that book right on his desk would make even the dumbest people notice his nasty ways.

"Settle down, class, and take your seats," said Dagner himself, standing at the front of the classroom. When everyone was seated, he said, "We will begin the lesson with a monster."

"But I thought that was Mr. Derek's job?" said a boy who Luke knew was John Davis. Mr. Derek was the Study of Beasts and Monsters teacher.

"Correct," Dagner replied. "Mr. Derek has asked me to teach you about this monster, however, due to the fact that he fears he will not get to it this year.

"Now, today I will be teaching you about a very fierce creature. It has the ability to create a storm of any kind with a mighty flap of its wings. This beast is called the *Thunderbird.*" Maddix saw Dagner's eyes flicker over to him for just a split-second; he was back to looking at the class.

"The Thunderbird," he continued, "has the face of a bird, and the legs of one. The body is larger than normal birds, but the wings are the feature that catches the eye.

The wingspan is 'larger than words themselves.' The eyes are beady and deadly."

Luke whispered to Maddix, "The rocket is launching." He left the room and went into a janitor's closet. Picking up a mop, he grinned. He turned invisible using his power and ran back to Dagner's classroom. Dagner himself was teaching his students about a Thunderbird's weakness.

"Thunderbirds are afraid of light and anything that has to do with it," he was saying, "so a candle, a lamp, or a light bulb would scare them half to death." Again, Dagner's eyes flickered over to Maddix. Was he wondering which thing he'd used to escape? Or did he somehow know already?

Meanwhile, Luke was stationed right behind Dagner, mop in hand. Maddix was the only person (besides Luke himself, of course) who knew this, however; if anyone— like the class—looked behind the Mythology teacher now, all they would see was a mop. And they did.

"Mr. Dagner?" a little girl named Kelsey Peterson asked nervously. "Was that mop there before?" Luke had crept, unnoticed, into the classroom, so no one had seen a lonely mop walking.

Luke held his breath as Dagner turned around. "The janitor must've left it here," he said, in barely more than a whisper. The students had a hard time hearing him, as he wasn't facing them. "I'll tell him." He didn't seem that convincing. He sniffed and moved forward; Luke sucked in his stomach.

"Let us get back to the lesson," he turned back around to face the class. Luke breathed a sigh of relief.

Near the end of the lesson, Dagner finally seemed to notice Luke's absence. Well, he must've noticed it sooner, but had to wait to address it. As the students were looking over their notes, Dagner made his way to Maddix.

"Where is Vincent?" he asked. Maddix again wondered why he called everybody by their last name. It was probably an evil thing.

"He left," Maddix said, having practiced it with Luke at lunch. "Had to deliver something to his dad—you know, the person in charge of this school." Dagner narrowed his eyes at him, his lips pursed.

"Very well," he said. "When will he return?"

Maddix was expecting this. "He should be back soon."

Dagner looked like he was about to question him further, but thought better of it. Without a word, he walked back to his desk.

With five minutes left in the lesson, Luke made his move. As Dagner was reading his *Sneak Attacks* book at his desk, Luke picked up the mop and hit him on the head. Dagner whirled around, rubbing a big lump on his scalp. He made a grab for the mop, as Luke knew he would, so Luke carried it away. He ran to the other side of the classroom. Dagner was chasing him—*And,* Maddix thought, *looking stupid while doing it.* His face looking murderous, Dagner made furious swipes toward both Luke and the mop. Luke was having so much fun, dodging an angry teacher. Maddix called, "It's okay, Mr. Dagner, I got it!" and Luke let him catch him.

"It's really quite easy, you know," Maddix said in an innocent, sweet voice. "I don't know *what* could've been a problem." He tapped the mop, making it appear like like he was using magic, and Luke carried it out of the classroom and back into the janitor's office. Then, he turned himself visible again, and walked back into the room. He went over to Dagner and asked, "Mr. Dagner, are you okay? Your face is a little red." Dagner looked like he could break both of Luke's arms off at once, while kicking him in the gut—but he didn't get a chance to do that, however; Maddix and Luke ran out of the room, stifling laughs.

During dinner, they told Nicole all about it. She was furious.

"You could've been caught!" she exclaimed. "Dagner could've made you do things that you wish you could forget! I'm really serious. Why would you do such a thing to an innocent teacher? What has he ever done to you?"

"Oh, I don't know," Maddix said, in mock concentration, "chuck me into a mirror, perhaps? Or be mean and creepy?"

"And relax, Nicole," Luke said to her. "Dagner's not gonna catch us; he could barely catch the mop I was holding."

"Well you boys can't come crying to me when you get punished!" Nicole cried. "And trust me, you will!" And, with that, she marched away from the table.

"Don't know what she's talking about," Luke said to Maddix in the hallway, walking back to their bedroom. "No one's going to know about that prank we played on Dagner."

"Shh," Maddix told him. "Not so loud, someone might hear—"

He was cut off by an approaching (and smirking) Dagner. He looked as malicious as ever, crossing his arms. "Oh, this is going to be good."

CHAPTER 17
EXPECTATIONS

D id you fulfill my requirements? Did you carry out the plan?"

Zennith shuffled his feet nervously as Sidero approached him.

"Yes," he said, "but—"

"But *what?*"

"But he found out," Zennith blurted out, "again."

"He's getting faster," Sidero tapped his chin.

"You're—you're not mad about the chip?" Zennith asked, surprised.

"In a way," Sidero answered. "You have failed me twice now, and that needs to continue."

"Continue?" Zennith repeated blankly. "Don't you want it to stop?"

"Of course, if I didn't see the beauty of it!" Sidero clapped his hands together. "Don't you *see*, Zennith? If we keep doing this, he'll either grow paranoid that he's going to be visited by you every night, or he'll grow overconfident that you'll either fail or be thwarted by him."

"But he's got a smart one on his side," Zennith pointed out. "That Rader girl. She's made of good stock."

"Yes," Sidero tapped his chin again, walking a few steps away. "We need to do something about that... has Lucian gotten out of it?"

The abrupt change of subject startled Zennith. "Gotten out of what?"

"The conversation," Sidero explained. "Parker would obviously tell that Vincent kid's father about his encounter with the—Thunderbirds, right? And I *still* don't know how Lucian contacted them—I heard they'd retreated to the Black Forest."

"He could've chosen smarter beasts, too," Zennith's brow was furrowed. "The fact that he chose Thunderbirds—Cacklefront and Fielderlow, for that matter—troubles me. He has better allies."

"Of course he does," Sidero replied. "Maybe he's hiding something."

"Yes," Zennith said, relieved that Sidero had finally felt what he'd been feeling. "What on Earth was that 'stage four' nonsense about?"

"Whatever it is, I hardly think it's nonsense," Sidero noticed the hint of worry in his voice, and quickly got rid of it. "But never fear; I'll question him sooner or later."

"It better be sooner. With his past..."

"I am fully aware of his past, Zennith," Sidero said.

Zennith didn't answer.

"I repeat: Do you understand me? We can't let the prophecy take place!"

Zennith looked right into Sidero's eyes and said, "Yes, I understand."

He understood the lengths of the prophecy very well.

CHAPTER 18
INTERROGATION

T his particular situation," Dagner said, circling around Maddix and Luke in his office, "is very interesting."

"So you think it was us?" Luke blurted out.

"Oh, I *know* it was you," Dagner said nastily. "Who else would do such a terrible—and poorly planned, I might add—trick?"

Luke opened his mouth, probably to say that it wasn't poorly planned, but Maddix kicked him, and he shut it.

"But what I must know," Dagner said, smirking, "is *why*. Had I *not* done anything to you except treat you with utmost respect?"

"The mirror!" the words escaped Maddix's mouth before he could stop them. "You pushed me in!"

"Ah, you know?" Dagner stroked his chin. "Most interesting. Listen: what you saw down there in the mirror was a figment of your imagination." Maddix folded his arms.

"And how do you know *that*?" he asked. "Hmm, by *sending* those Thunderbirds down there?"

"Yes, that reminds me," Dagner bent down and faced Maddix, who was terrified. Luke just stared blankly. "How *did* you escape?"

"With pure wits and smarts," Maddix glared right into his eyes.

"So you won't tell me?" Dagner stood up again. "Very well. But let me remind you, Parker, that you and Vincent here are in a sticky situation, in which I have the upper hand. Now, let me ask you again: How did you escape?"

Maddix knew he'd cornered them for this, so he could question him about this, even if it was right in front of Luke. He wasn't going to fall for it, though. Not this time.

He stayed silent.

"You still won't tell me," Dagner said. "Well, that is going to change."

Maddix didn't know what to make of that. *That's going to change?* He thought. *Yeah, right. And I'm the President of the United States.* But the thought still nagged at him; *could* that change?

No, he wasn't going to be vulnerable anymore. He was going to stand his ground.

"That is never going to change," he said, "so unless you can find a way to get into my mind, stop trying. You're going to fail." He didn't know how he'd thought of it; the words just came spilling out of his mouth, one by one.

"Actually, *I* won't be the one going into your mind," Dagner snarled. "*You* will."

Luke gulped and turned invisible. Dagner hadn't forgotten him, though.

"I know you're there," Dagner said. He grabbed Luke's arm and steered him outside.

"We'll be just a minute," Dagner told Luke, as he turned back toward Maddix. Increasingly worried, Luke closed the door.

"You can't make me talk," Maddix said.

"Oh?" Dagner raised his eyebrows. "I had the impression I could."

Suddenly, he was gone. The lights were off, and Maddix was alone.

CHAPTER 19
CRIMINAL MINDS

Dagner appeared in the valley, hot, but pleased. He approached two figures in the distance. He said, "Hello." One of the them jumped in surprise.

"Lucian!" Zennith pulled his scarf away from his face and studied Dagner.

"Good to see you too, Zennith," Dagner said, stretching out a hand. Zennith shook it, looking into Dagner's eyes. Lucian looked extremely satisfied. What was he so happy about?

"Lucian," the other figure tore his scarf from his face, revealing Sidero's mean features, "you have news?"

"Of course," Dagner bowed. Straightening up, he said, "I've just been with Parker. Asked him about—"

"Wait a minute," Zennith interrupted. Ignoring both Sidero's and Dagner's disapproving faces, he asked, "How'd you get him alone?"

"He actually gave me the perfect opportunity," Dagner said, grinning. His grin faded. "Alas, that opportunity came at a price: he and his friend had played a little trick on me—a trick sinister enough to get them into trouble. Well, a little more than just enough, but still—you can't always get what you want. Anyway, he and his friend were in my office, and that Vincent boy seemed more afraid than Parker himself. So, I dismissed him. I didn't want him to interfere with the questioning."

"You...?" Zennith's eyes went wide, unable to finish the sentence.

"No, he didn't kill him," Sidero waved in his servant's direction. "Honestly, Zennith, what is with you and killing these days?" He turned back to Dagner. "Go on, Lucian."

"Well, I asked Parker directly how he'd escaped the Thunderbirds," Dagner continued, "and he wouldn't tell me—I'd expected this, of course. He probably knew I was evil from the start. So, I switched to Plan B. I extinguished the room's lights and left him alone to deal with himself."

"You left him alone?" Sidero repeated. "But he could escape! He probably has weapons with him!"

"Would a boy his age carry weapons around in his pockets?" Dagner asked. "But, trust me, if he had any magical weapons, they were turned off and unusable. He's stuck."

"Wonderful," Sidero said, clapping. "Absolutely wonderful. However, when you let him out, what will happen afterwards?"

"I've got a plan for that, too," Dagner said.

"Before you leave, Lucian," Zennith said, stepping towards him. "May I ask what stage four of your plan is?"

"Stage four is me teleporting back to Apollo to set a few traps," Dagner said. "My time was cut short, of course, because he escaped from the Thunderbirds. Even still, I was able to set a couple traps."

"Perfect," Sidero said. "You may leave, Lucian."

And, with that, Dagner turned on the spot and vanished.

CHAPTER 20
THOUGHTS

Maddix considered his position. He figured Dagner was still in the room somewhere. He was alone... in a dark room... with an evil man... who wanted something from him.

"I know you're there!" he called out.

There was no reply. Maddix wondered how he was going to get out of there—obviously, he wasn't going to tell Dagner about how he'd escaped the grasp (it was a very un-proffesional grasp, but still a grasp) of the Thunderbirds. Then, it came to him: how he'd escaped! The Electro Pencil! Maddix fished around in his pocket and extracted it. He turned it on, and lifted it high into the air, just as he had done in the chute with Cacklefront and Fielderlow. Expecting electric beams, Maddix grinned and looked up... but none came. Slowly, he brought it down, examining it. Could it be broken? Or could Dagner have rigged it to not work?

"Ah, come on!" Maddix shouted into the dark. Then, his tone got worried. "What should I do, what should I do?" He brought out his notepad and a regular pencil, and wrote down his thoughts, even though he could only faintly make out the words in the dark.

Okay, so I'm stuck in a dark room and Dagner has the upper hand.
Hmmm...probably NOT the best place to be. Let's see...I could use my powers to—to what? I can't use my powers to get me out of this, I can only read minds. What good does that do when I'm the only person in the room? But wait—what if Dagner's here too? Nah, he would've made a sound. Or I would've heard him breathing. Let me check...

Maddix paused, straining his ears for a breath, a footfall—any sign of life. Nothing.

Moving on. Maybe I COULD tell Dagner how I escaped. I mean, it's a small price to pay for—whatever's happening. I could probably get out of here if I told him that I'd used an Electro Pencil to get out of the chute. Oh, geez, I hope he doesn't look in my pockets. He probably will—he thinks of everything. Well, he WOULD find out one way or another, I would just be getting it over with faster if I told him...

"What am I *saying?*" he asked aloud. Then, he went back to writing.

No, DON'T tell him. He'd go ballistic with joy. Bet Dagner'd go straight to Sidero and tell him. How would he find the time? Better make him wait. What if he got SO angry with how long he'd have to wait, he'd just give up on me? Nah, that's a stupid plan. What if I just ignore him and don't answer when he asks me again (which he probably will)? He'd torture me. And what do I know, anyway? Dagner's unpredictable. What if, as soon as he came back, I used my powers to know what's coming? He'd probably see THAT coming. Didn't Fielderlow say something about closing your mind? Dagner'd probably know how to do that, and he'd block me out. I need more time...

Maddix tapped his pencil against the pad, and then broke it. Regretting it at once, he picked up the pieces and put them in his pocket. He took deep breaths, and said, "Just stay calm, just stay calm, just stay calm..."

He wrote it down with a different pencil.

Just stay calm, just stay calm, just stay calm...

The pencil tip snapped. Maddix placed that in his pocket, along with the notepad. He kept taking deep breaths and looked around, trying to see through the darkness. Suddenly, there was a flash of light.

"Time's up," said a voice.

CHAPTER 21
INTERCEPTION

B reathtaking," Sidero said, looking around.

"What—the view?" Zennith asked.

"No," Sidero turned back to him. "Lucian's plan."

"Yes," Zennith agreed. "But—forgive me if I'm not being rational—it's a bit... bit creepy."

"I see your point," Sidero nodded. "When you said that he rose to the occasion magnificently, I think he rose to it *too* magnificently."

"That whole 'deal with himself' thing, right?" Zennith smiled now that Sidero and he had similar opinions. "He scares me a little bit."

"Understandable," Sidero was smiling now, "the weak are sometimes vulnerable to more powerful men."

"What?" Zennith said, his eyes wide. "Wait—"

"I know, I know," Sidero laughed. "You are neither vulnerable nor weak."

"Thank you!" Zennith said. When he saw Sidero's smile falter, he added, "Sir."

"Good," Sidero said, stepping away. "Now, I want you to make another visit to Apollo Academy."

"Why?" Zennith asked.

"I need you to spy on Parker," Sidero stripped off his gloves and threw them into the distance.

"Why'd you do that?" Zennith asked him. "They were perfectly good gloves."

"It's a way of telling people that victory is imminent here," Sidero said.

CHAPTER 22
TO TALK OR NOT TO TALK?

I will ask you this one more time," Dagner said, pushing the lantern's light to Maddix, "what did you do to escape from the Thunderbirds?"

Maddix stayed silent, looking right into Dagner's eyes. He tried making the DWAH face, but Dagner just laughed.

"No, I'm afraid that's not going to work," he said. "So consider your options: Answer me, or I'll *make you.*"

Maddix's nostrils flared, and his eyes got wide. What will he do if he didn't answer? All he could think of was—

"I—didn't escape. I just—left."

"Left?" Dagner repeated. "They let you go?"

"No," Maddix said. "I—got smart."

"And you left," Dagner said, "while they tried to stop you?"

"Yeah," Maddix said, feeling dumber by the second.

"So that's basically escaping," Dagner said coolly.

"Sure?" Maddix just stared at him, feeling hopeless. He couldn't use his powers, he didn't have a plan, and Dagner was thinking (more than he already did) that he was incredibly stupid.

"Okay, then," Dagner snapped. The lights flickered on. "Let's try something else."

The lights were off again. Maddix heard a scuffling noise. The lights turned on. Dagner had his notepad.

"Interesting," he said, reading its contents. "You heard my conversation with Mr. Vincent the other day?"

Maddix nodded. "Yeah, I did. And you can't make me forget what I heard."

"Okay," Dagner stepped back. He flipped to another page. "Ah, yes. Here are my answers."

Maddix gulped. Had he found his entry about how he'd escaped?

The answer was yes. Yes, he had.

"An Electro Pencil," Dagner said. "Most astonishing. Those are almost impossible to find, let alone hold. How on earth did you get your hands on it?"

"You've already found out more than you should have," Maddix said. "I'm not giving you any more information."

"Fine," Dagner replied. He snapped the notepad shut.

"How long are you going to keep me here?" Maddix asked.

"Just a few more minutes," Dagner told him.

Or years, Maddix thought. He stared right into Dagner's cold eyes. The Mythology teacher stared right back. Maddix then saw a single ray of hope, and said it aloud.

"You can't prove I did anything wrong."

"Oh, really?" Dagner asked. He turned to the small blackboard behind him and started writing things as he spoke. "You have *continually* used your powers."

"So?" Maddix asked, not seeing what was wrong.

"You are eleven," Dagner wrote the number on the board. "But, you are supposed to be *sixteen* to use your powers." He wrote the number sixteen above the eleven and wrote the minus sign. He did the equation and said, "So, you are *five years* ahead of schedule. That is a very bad thing. If people—and by people, I mean the magical government—know about this, you will be severely punished."

Maddix gulped.

"But, if you tell me *in full detail* what happened between you and the Thunderbirds, I'll consider avoiding the subject."

Maddix's hands were sweating. The magical government? Who were they? What would happen if Dagner told them that he'd been underage and using his powers? Would they arrest a kid?

And, if he told Dagner the details of his escape, would Dagner keep his promise? Or would he tell the government anyway?

All these questions whirred inside his head, chasing each other around.

"What will it be?" Dagner walked back to him.

"So, to recap, you played a prank on Dagner, he got you into trouble, and is threatening you to either tell him how you escaped the Thunderbirds or he'll tell the magical government?" Nicole asked.

"Yeah, that's pretty much it." Maddix said.

They were with Luke in Nicole's bedroom, ~~helping~~ watching Nicole do her homework. Maddix and Luke had just finished telling her about their eventful day.

"And where were *you* in all of this?" Luke said, glaring at her. "Going to your classes and learning stuff?"

"Isn't that the point of school?" Nicole asked.

"Well, you weren't helping us get out of trouble!" Luke exclaimed, pointing a furious finger at her.

"Luke, how was I supposed to know that you were in trouble?" Nicole said. "And, if I'd somehow known, I couldn't've just barged right into Dagner's office and said, 'Hey, you need to let my friends go or you'll answer to me!'"

"That's exactly what you should've done!" Luke exploded.

"Calm down, Luke," Maddix said. "Nicole's done her best."

"Which is *nothing*!" Luke shouted. "She's been just sitting here, being mad at us!"

"I'm not mad at you," Nicole said, "I'm just—disappointed."

"Disappointed?" Luke repeated. "*I'm* disappointed in *you* for not coming to our aid when we needed it most!"

"Luke," Nicole said, chewing on her lip. "I'm *really* sorry I couldn't have been there, but I wasn't. The point is, you and Maddix didn't get hurt."

"What if we had?" Luke said. "I'm serious, Nicole. The *one* time we needed you—"

Nicole glared at him, all sense of pity or regret gone. "Luke, let it go! And plus, that wasn't the *one time you needed me*—what about the time you were fighting my fake dad *who was a griffin*? Didn't you need me a lot then?"

"But—I—ah!" Luke jumped out of his seat and flung his arms out.

"Breathe, Luke," Maddix placed his hands on his friend's shoulders. "Just breathe."

Luke was breathing fast, looking at Nicole. "You make me *so mad* sometimes!" He made to grab at her; Nicole stepped back.

"Are—are you really Luke Vincent?" she asked nervously.

"What are you talking about?" Maddix said, pulling Luke away as he lunged at Nicole.

137

"He could be an imposter, like—like Sirien was," she said, stammering slightly. She walked to the door and closed it.

"I don't think so," Maddix said. "I was with him the whole day."

"Was there a point that he *wasn't* with you?" Nicole asked urgently.

Maddix wracked his brain. He'd been standing out of Dagner's door when Dagner had interrogated him privately! And Maddix had been wondering why he hadn't just looked through the window and rushed in to help him. Either he'd been replaced, or Dagner had done something to the windows so that he couldn't see through them.

Maddix told Nicole about it.

"Get a Truth Light," Nicole said hurriedly.

"A what?" Maddix asked, looking around. Luke was going wild; he was throwing things at the walls.

"A Truth Light," Nicole pointed to the dresser. "That—that flashlight on my dresser! Turn it on and point it on Luke! Ask, 'Are you an imposter of Luke Vincent?'"

"Okay," Maddix said, thinking about how bizarre—yet brilliant—a Truth Light was. He grabbed the flashlight and shined its light on Luke, who was making his way towards Nicole's desk.

"Are you an imposter of Luke Vincent?" he asked.

There was a shattering noise; the lights were off and on again, only to reveal a hawk-like face looking right at them.

"Did you miss me?"

CHAPTER 23
COMEBACK

W hat I'm about to tell you to do is dangerous," Dagner paced up in down in front of his allies, the old factory's cobblestone floors hard and rough against his feet.

"Dangerous?" squeaked the smaller of the two. "Are-are you sure you want *us* to do this job?"

"Yes," Dagner said. "Don't you want to get revenge?"

"On him?" the smaller creature said. "You said it had to do with him."

"Of course it has to do with him!" Dagner exclaimed. He calmed down. "Now, I need *you* to go undercover as someone close to him…"

"Me?" the small one asked. "Why me?"

"Because," Dagner said, "if something goes wrong, they'll get rid of you."

"Hey!" Cacklefront shouted.

"Calm down," Dagner said, "I was only joking." He turned to the bigger one. "Fielderlow, I need you to kidnap—let's see here—Mr. Vincent's son, Lukas. Hide him somewhere in the school. Then use your Invisi-Ray to make yourself invisible so you can sneak around the room where Cacklefront will reveal himself. Attack when they'll never see it coming."

Fielderlow nodded, while Cacklefront looked perplexed.

"I'll reveal myself?" he asked.

"Yes," Dagner told him. "Either you'll do it by yourself, or Parker and that Rader girl will figure it out before you get the chance. Whichever way works."

"So what you're saying is," Cacklefront said, "I have to make myself vulnerable to a couple of kids? Wait, let me rephrase that: I have to make myself vulnerable to a couple of kids with *superpowers*?"

"Superpowers they can't use until they are sixteen," Dagner smirked. "And I can always just randomly enter the scene and tell them off for using their powers if they do. Just call me."

"What will stop them from defeating me and Fielderlow besides you just walking in and telling them not to?" Cacklefront asked.

"Trust me, they'll stop using their powers when I walk in," Dagner said. "Just watch."

CHAPTER 24
THE RETURN OF THE THUNDERBIRDS

Cacklefront walked towards them, his eyes alight with a fire that Maddix couldn't explain. It was revenge, anger, and a hint of fear. And—was that *shame?*

"Well, well, well," the Thunderbird took out a large, gleaming sword and scraped the floor with it. "If it isn't Maddix Parker."

"Cacklefront," Maddix said, glaring at him. His fingers flew to his pocket, where the Electro Pencil rested. "I can beat you once, and I can beat you again. Is Fielderlow here, too?"

"Is he?" Cacklefront looked around, not worriedly, but mockingly. "Or isn't he?"

Maddix looked around the room frantically. Fielderlow was the smarter of the two; if he was here, Maddix was dead for sure. *Well,* Maddix thought, *this time at least I know where I am.*

Nicole tugged on his arm. She whispered, "Maddix, who is this?"

"Cacklefront," Maddix whispered back, "a Thunderbird."

Her face turned pale. "I've read about them. They're supposed to be *really* dangerous."

"I know," Maddix said. "But I can beat him." *Hopefully.*

He turned to Cacklefront, who had been watching them.

"Not scared, are you?" he said, smirking. "'Cause the people who are scared aren't usually the heroes."

"Well this one is," Maddix said. He took out the Electro Pencil, held it up high, and said to Nicole, "Sorry about your room, but I've gotta do this to live."

Electric beams shot up from the pencil's tip, but they stopped abruptly. Maddix brought it down, confused.

"Huh?"

"Guess your Electro Pencil doesn't work now," Cacklefront jeered. "I made sure you can't use more than five seconds' worth of powers in this room."

Five seconds... he only had five seconds of power? *Well,* he thought, *better use it wisely.* Hoping desperately that Cacklefront had meant five seconds each power, he screwed up his face and made the DWAH face, looking right at the Thunderbird.

"Not gonna work," Cacklefront said, his smirk getting wider. Maddix saw dancing flames—but something was

143

wrong. A huge wave of water came crashing down onto it, and the next thing he knew, Maddix was on the floor.

"What… what happened?"

"You fell," Nicole said, hurrying over to him.

"I know *that*," Maddix said, standing up. "But why?"

"Did you see anything?" Nicole asked him.

"Yeah," Maddix replied, "the fire—which comes right before my mind-reading power—was extinguished by tons of water."

"As it should have," Cacklefront raised a hand, and Maddix slammed against the wall. "I've got real power now, and you can't stop me."

Nicole mustered up enough courage to say, "You'll have to get through me to get to him."

"Oh, really?" Cacklefront asked, advancing. "Or do I just have to do—this!" He raised his hand again, and Nicole was blasted to the other side of the room.

"Whoa!" Maddix said, getting up from the floor. Just then, an idea popped into his head. "You've got some pretty awesome powers there, Cacklefront. I don't know why I thought I could *possibly* stop you."

He saw the old gleam in the Thunderbird's eye; Maddix knew that he was bursting to talk about it further. Maddix kept going.

"And I won't even *start* about your wings. Did you make them stronger? I bet you could make fiercer storms in a heartbeat."

"Think you can flatter me to defeat, Parker?" the Thunderbird asked, after a pause.

"I guess it's my only option," Maddix gave a huge, fake sigh. "You've got the upper hand, and here I am standing here praising you. Guess I should stop—"

"Don't stop!" Cacklefront blurted out. Maddix smiled.

"You *don't* want me to stop?" Maddix asked, putting on a look of fake concern.

"No, don't!" Cacklefront exclaimed. Then he cleared his throat. "I mean, no, don't stop—because it doesn't work on me! Does—does that make sense? Or is it—you know what, forget it."

Suddenly, Nicole screamed. Maddix whirled around to see the cause of it. He gasped as he saw it: another Thunderbird, much smarter than the other, with a falcon-like face and slightly sharper talons.

"Fielderlow!" Cacklefront said weakly. "What took you so long?"

"You're welcome for rescuing you," Fielderlow rolled his eyes.

"You've been in the room the whole time?" Maddix asked.

"Yeah," Fielderlow turned to him. "Waiting for just the right moment to *destroy you*."

"He could've blown me to pieces!" Cacklefront exclaimed.

Fielderlow looked at Maddix "Him? No, you've got nothing to worry about." Cacklefront was about to protest when Nicole squeaked from the wall, "Um—Mr. Fielderlow, sir, how were you in the room the whole time? We certainly would've noticed you."

"Quiet," Fielderlow said sharply, and Nicole fell silent at once. "But, all the same, I used an Invisi-Ray 3000. It's a new model that also stifles sound. I could be stomping the whole time—in fact, I was—and you wouldn't hear it." Nicole nodded.

"And now," Fielderlow turned back to Maddix, "to business."

"Ooh, are you gonna force him to talk?" Cacklefront asked.

"Yes," Fielderlow responded. "And you can't stop me, Parker."

Maddix immediately fixed Fielderlow with the DWAH face and saw dancing flames. He entered Fielderlow's mind once more and saw his thoughts. He saw a flash of a thought that looked like: *Where are you, Dagner? The boy's using his powers. He's right where we want him.*

What? Maddix had a sinking feeling. He'd fallen right into their trap! And apparently Dagner was supposed to come in any second—

There was a flash of light, and he was back in the bedroom. And sure enough, there was a knock on the door and Dagner came in.

"Hello?" he said. "What are you doing?"

Maddix had an idea who he was talking to. Nicole, apparently, didn't.

"Mr. Dagner, sir, they're attacking us!" she exclaimed, forgetting in the heat of the moment Dagner was, himself, evil. But, to her, any teacher arriving on the scene would restore order. Unfortunately, that wasn't true.

"Attacking you? Who's attacking you?" Dagner looked around. "I don't see anyone."

"What?" Maddix said. He turned around; Cacklefront and Fielderlow had disappeared. The Invisi-Ray!

"Sir, they're using an Invisi-Ray," Maddix said. "And I think you know what that is."

"Please, believe us," Nicole pleaded. "I know we've gotten on the wrong side of you, but please!"

The wrong side of him? Maddix thought. *Man, she's desperate.*

"Were you using your powers at all?" Dagner asked. Maddix's heart dropped; this was the plan. He was in trouble now.

When there was no answer, Dagner said, "Were you?"

Nicole's gulp was audible.

"Well," he said, "that's a problem."

CHAPTER 25
THE PROPHECY

Just make sure you aren't seen until you're supposed to be," came Zennith's voice. There was a rustling sound and Zennith reappeared in the doorway.

"You sent them off?" Sidero asked.

"Yes," Zennith sunk down onto the floor. "And good riddance, too."

"Don't speak ill of the beasts, Zennith, when you yourself have been slacking." Sidero's words came out as if his voice were a snake's.

"Sir?" Zennith stepped closer. "Sir, are you alright?" His master hadn't been like this since the War of Moaren; or, more recently, since the re-discovery of Maddix Parker.

"He— he's getting to me," Sidero shook himself. "The boy."

Zennith's eyes went wide as he understood. "The prophecy?"

Sidero nodded.

Zennith quickly extracted a very worn piece of parchment from his pocket: a prophecy written many years ago.

"You carry that around with you?" Sidero ask him. "What for?"

"Oh, you know. Banquets, dinners, speeches," Zennith shrugged. "And it never hurt anyone to take a peek once in awhile."

"A peek?" Sidero said. "Oh, so you're just *wishing* for my downfall?"

"Oh, no, sir," Zennith stepped back, offended. "Of course not, sir. I've been merely checking to see its order."

"Its order," Sidero repeated. "Okay."

"May I?" Zennith asked. Sidero nodded again.

Zennith read: "*Evil is growing, its forces gaining, the power of the dark, and all things remaining. As the clouds block the sun, the dark blocks the light, and the bad and the good all resort to a fight.*

But when all is lost, when hope is diminished, evil will be done, over, finished. For the light in the dark has entered at last, a boy with the mind that shatters the glass. And as years pass, and the boy turns twelve, evil's last standing will never be held."

"He's eleven now," Sidero said, pacing. "We're running out of time."

Zennith studied the parchment. "'A boy with the mind shatters the glass.' He can read minds—that's his power! We've gotta close our minds before he—"

"Before he *what*, though?" Sidero wondered aloud. "What on Earth is 'shattering the glass?'"

"Is it literal?" Zennith suggested. "He could actually break glass."

"No, I don't think it's literal," Sidero shook his head. "Wrack your brains and see if you can remember a metaphor involving glass."

There was silence as the two beings started to think.

"Oh!" Zennith said after a minute or so. "It could mean he's breaking something strong—an inanimate object, like trust or peace."

"Brilliant!" Sidero exclaimed. "But what is he breaking?"

"I think I've got it," Zennith said. He whispered it to Sidero.

"Get ready, Zennith," he said, "this is going to be dangerous."

CHAPTER 26
IN TROUBLE

L isten to us, please. The Thunderbirds—"

"I don't want any explanations," Dagner said shortly, as he marched them to his office. "I know you've used your powers and—as I've said—that's a quite serious problem."

"Sir, what you don't understand is a lot," Nicole said. Maddix thought, *Nicole, nothing good ever happens when you start a sentence like that!* And that was exactly what happened.

"No, what *you* don't understand is a lot," Dagner said. "And I want you to listen to me: Thunderbirds don't exist—"

"*They don't exist?*" Maddix threw his head back and laughed. "They don't exist? Thunderbirds don't exist? Are you *kidding me*? You asked me—you directly asked me— how I'd escape them! And now—"

"And now I need you to listen to the end of my sentence," Dagner was so serious that Maddix stepped back. "I said that Thunderbirds don't exist in this part of the world. So, how could you have seen them here?"

"Sir," Maddix was back to being desperate. "But, sir, you just don't know what we saw." He and Nicole sat down in chairs in Dagner's office.

"I know all about what you saw," Dagner's words came as a shock to Maddix and Nicole.

"You do?"

"Of course," Dagner stood up. He walked to the chalkboard and pulled down a screen. It showed a projector. He had been prepared for this. "Holograms are projected from afar—usually from a bush or a large nearby object—and they show anything the person projecting it wishes it to show. Let's say it's me and I want you to see—hmm—Thunderbirds, then I would use the projector to project a holographic image of Thunderbirds. It just so happens that I know which Thunderbirds you 'saw.'"

"You know Cacklefront and Fielderlow?" Maddix gasped. This proves he was on their side! He can't find a loophole now! Unless...

"I researched them when I was in college, studying the Mythological Arts," he said. "And I saw that they are highly dangerous—especially to children. I suggest you stay away from them—holograms or not, you never know. Look out for them."

"You said 'holograms or not'?" Maddix said. "Well, how do you know that these Thunderbirds *weren't* holograms?"

He was surprised when Nicole answered.

"Because… he was there," she interjected. "I saw him crouching by Luke's bed when Cacklefront blasted me. He went out when Cacklefront was saying how you could've hurt him."

"He said that?" Dagner's tone was different than before.

"Yeah," Maddix said, getting an idea. "Yeah, and if you don't take us seriously and tell us what's going on, I'll follow up on that."

Dagner shook himself both mentally and visibly. "No, I don't think that's going to happen." He started walking to his desk.

"Why not?" Maddix asked.

"Because," his finger hovered over a button on his desk, "you'll be joining your friend."

And he pushed it.

CHAPTER 27
CRYSTAL BALL

Fire licked the wood in the fireplace of an abandoned house. Sidero and Zennith were sitting at a table, discussing plans.

"You'll be with the projector?" Sidero asked.

"Yes," Zennith responded. "Lucian said to turn on the projector *after*—and only after—Parker, Rader, and Vincent have reunited."

"Yes, I remember," Sidero nodded. "And you'll project—?"

"Lucian himself," Zennith said. "Laughing, cackling. It'll give us time."

"To what?" Sidero was testing him, looking to see if he was taking it as seriously as he was.

"To see if Parker has—whatever we're looking for," Zennith said, looking around the house, making sure it was indeed abandoned. "You're sure this is quite empty?"

"I am sure," Sidero replied. "It once belonged to Derek Garder, the husband of Lydia."

"The one in charge of Wolfby High?" Zennith asked. "Yes, I know her. The school's in competition with Apollo."

"Quite right," Sidero turned back to the plans. "Let see… oh yes, do you remember what to do after he reveals his powers of friendship? We advance on him."

"And if he doesn't?"

"We fall back and keep watching till it's over."

"And if we have to keep throwing things at him until he shows his friendship powers?"

"We keep throwing things at him until he shows his friendship powers."

Sidero grinned. "Precisely. Now, let me look in the crystal ball…"

"The crystal ball?" Zennith asked, taken aback. "That's a little fortune-teller for you, Sidero."

"Yes, I expect so," Sidero replied, but he took the mist-filled ball out just the same. He looked into its depths and after a minute or so he exclaimed, "Look! I see him." Zennith crouched down beside him and peered into the mist.

"Yes, there he is," he said, seeing Maddix and Nicole falling in the darkness. "Ah, Lucian, always with the falling in darkness. It's just like last time, although Parker isn't alone now."

"Maybe," Sidero looked up and at his servant, "maybe that is a problem."

"No," Zennith shook his head. "It's better, actually."

Sidero stroked his chin. "I guess," he said. He looked back at the crystal ball. "Watch out, Parker—we're coming for you."

His and Zennith's evil laughs echoed throughout the room.

CHAPTER 28
EXPECTANT

Nicole's screams echoed, so Maddix thought they were falling in some enclosed space.

"Nicole, scream again," he said, trying to veer to the far right, far enough to hit something solid.

"Okay," Nicole said, and she shrieked, high and shrill.

"You can stop now," Maddix said, clutching his ears as he made his way to the right. "You're giving me a headache."

"Sorry," Nicole said, "it's just—how are you so used to it? You seem so calm."

"Well, I've been through this recently," Maddix told her, "and I'm trying to get us back on solid ground. That is, before it hits us first." He backed up, then rammed his shoulder into—thin air. Or *was* it thin? Maddix sniffed; it smelled musty, like wherever they were had old rust in it. Finally, he hit something! But what was it?

"Nicole, try to—ugh—veer to the—urgh!—left," he said, mustering enough force to break the solid bar or platform or whatever it was right in half. *That's it— platform!* Maddix thought. *This could be another garbage shoot!* He sniffed again; it still smelled musty—not like garbage. But then again, did the garbage shoot actually *smell* like garbage? Maddix thought back to his first encounter with the Thunderbirds. He had been so scared he hadn't stopped to think, let alone smell the air. He turned back to Nicole, who was edging to the left, but kept flying back.

"Here, let me help you," he said, and he grabbed Nicole's arm and lead her to the far left. There was a *thud!*

Nicole turned quickly to Maddix. "What's that?"

"I don't know," Maddix shrugged. "Go find out." Nicole punched it, and drew her hand back.

"It's definitely solid," she said. "But what *is* it?"

Maddix was just saying, "I don't know," when her eyes went wide.

"Do you still have the Truth Light?" she asked. Maddix's mind went blank. *The what?* Then, he remembered: Cacklefront replacing Luke, him battling Cacklefront, Nicole seeing Dagner hunched against the bed… it seemed like ages ago. Then, a thought struck him. *Cacklefront replacing Luke…* that's it!

"Hey, Nicole!" Maddix exclaimed. "Didn't Dagner say we would be 'joining our friend?'"

"So we have to find Luke!" Nicole said, catching on. But her face fell instantly. "But—where is he?"

"At the bottom," Maddix said, "or on the way down."

"Maddix," Nicole said fearfully, "Maddix—what if there are more Thunderbirds here? Ones like Fielderlow? Smarter, even?"

Maddix now understood. Nicole was feeling expectant, a feeling you should never feel when you're falling down a very dark chute—or slide—or whatever this was. She was expecting large, scary beasts to rain down on them, all equipped with weapons and a battle plan. Or worse.

Maddix searched his pockets for the Truth Light. Nothing. He *did* find the Electro Pencil, though. He raised it high into the air, willing the electric beams to explode out of its tip. Seconds before he knew it would happen, he told Nicole, "Cover your face. This could get messy."

He closed his eyes, hoping so much that the electric beams would save them from the darkness, but there was nothing.

"Darn it," he said, bringing the pencil back down and placing it in his pocket once more. "This never works when I need it—except *one* time."

"Did you find the Truth Light?" Nicole asked him.

Maddix shook his head. "No, I—"

Suddenly, there was a rumbling sound and a creaking noise. A rough voice called, "Take the girl." Maddix tried to cover Nicole, but the person—or being—was too quick for him. Nicole was screaming again as she was hoisted into the air and swallowed by darkness.

"Nicole!" Maddix called. "Nicole, can you hear me?"

He took a distant scream as a reply.

"Use your secret weapons!" Maddix shouted. "Use them wisely!"

"Wisely, eh?" a sneer voice said. It sounded very close to Maddix. "And how would that play out?"

"What?" Maddix said, edging backwards.

"How would you use your 'secret weapons' wisely?" Whoever the sneer voice belonged to, they were getting closer by the second. "Would you use it against the enemy?"

Maddix gulped. "Yes."

"And who *is* the enemy?" the sneer voice asked. "Not us, hopefully?"

"Us?" Maddix said, not answering his question. He had two reasons for doing so: One, he was too scared to say yes, and two, because he wanted to know if the sneering being was alone.

Apparently not.

"All of *my kind*, that is," Maddix felt breath around him in the darkness—much more than one being could breathe. "You see, I've got a certain *job* to do, and I want to get it done."

"You—you do?" Maddix tried his best not to stutter; he wondered if the being could sense fear.

"Yes," the being was getting closer… and closer… and closer. "And don't play games with us, Parker, we've got our minds blocked and impenetrable. Isn't that a *problem* to you?" He put a lot of pressure and emphasis on the word, 'problem.'

Maddix didn't answer him. All he did was widen his eyes.

The being cackled. "Not scared, are you? 'Cause we might just attack—" His voice changed location quickly; Maddix flinched—"at any moment."

Something growled from behind him, and Maddix whipped around.

"Don't move," the first being said, "or there'll be problems."

CHAPTER 29
THE VIEW OF AN OUTSIDER

Every second counts, Zennith," Sidero said quietly, creeping along the metal floor.

"Yes, I know," Zennith replied, right behind his master. "And you're *sure* these are soundproof?"

"I'm quite sure," Sidero said, shifting to the side. "But it can be a pain at times. We don't want to miss all the fun."

Zennith strained his ears. Nothing. "Should Jackelhide be advancing by now?"

"Yes," Sidero nodded. "That manticore's got a mind of steel, sure, but he's milking it for all its worth."

"I get what you mean," Zennith said, grunting and moving further. "He loves his job a little too much if you ask me."

"Quite right," Sidero said. "But we need to focus on the pros here. After all, he *was* the only beast of his kind who was up for the job—or at least to be the leader. The rest: we literally had to to *force* them to fly here."

"And that leaves us crawling in the vents," Zennith muttered.

"Don't complain about the uncomfortable atmosphere," Sidero said, moving forward. "It'll be over soon."

"I guess you're right," Zennith said. And they were silent for the rest of the journey.

After ten minutes or so, Sidero stopped. Zennith almost bumped into him.

"What is it?"

"We're here," Sidero whispered. "Be quiet."

Zennith nodded as Sidero knocked on the metal plate right in front of him and it popped open.

There, they could see... nothing. It was all darkness. But they heard voices.

"... not scared, are you?" was the voice of Jackelhide. "Because we might just attack at any moment."

"Don't take out the flashlight," Sidero whispered as Zennith reached for it. "This is getting good."

There was a scuffling noise; had a fight broken out? No, one of Jackelhide's men (not exactly men, but "soldiers") had grabbed Parker and he had struggled. It wasn't exactly a *fight*, more like a *lunge*.

"Let go of me!" Parker yelled. But the manticore didn't let go; in fact, his grip tightened. "Ouch!"

"So, he's handling himself pretty well, isn't he?" Sidero said softly.

"Who, Jackelhide or Parker?" Zennith asked inquisitively.

"Both," Sidero replied. He turned to him. "And I'm surprised Parker hasn't used his powers yet."

"Jackelhide probably blocked his mind," Zennith said. "He thinks ahead. Things like that can be dangerous."

"Yes," Sidero said, turning back to the darkness. "Yes, I suppose so."

CHAPTER 30
LUNGES AND LAUNCHES

W hat are you, anyway?" Maddix asked. Despite his fear, he was very curious. He was sure the being couldn't have been another Thunderbird; maybe a griffin? Or possibly something much more dangerous.

"I am a manticore," it said proudly, "by the name of Jackelhide."

Jackelhide? What kind of name is that? Maddix thought, but in this situation, thinking about the name of a being that might kill you right at that moment is not a good idea. He bit his tongue to not say anything like this out loud.

Unfortunately, he bit his tongue too late.

"A manticore?" he said. "You're a *manticore?*"

"Yeah," Jackelhide said snidely, "got a problem with that?"

165

"It's just—you're—never mind," Maddix looked around. He decided to play the "super-annoying-kid-who-hates-everything-and-everyone" card.

"Can we land somewhere? I'm tired of falling," he said.

"Geez, you *are* stubborn," Jackelhide said. Maddix bit back a retort. He was *not*. There was a rustle of wings, and Maddix felt himself being pulled by the arms and dropped hard onto a hard surface—a *very* hard surface. He rubbed his head.

"Alright, we're not falling anymore," Jackelhide said, "tell us what we need and we'll consider letting you go." The last part seemed robotic, as if Jackelhide had rehearsed this many times.

"Go on," the manticore said. His tone was almost soft, but the sneer was still there. "Tell us everything we want to know, and we won't hurt you." But they already had; and who knows what they were doing to Nicole at the moment?

"W—what do you want?" Maddix asked, forgetting the card he was playing in this very dangerous game. He was back to fear.

Jackelhide seemed very pleased that his victim was scared, and he replied with less softness, more sneer. But it seemed very much that he was trying hard to keep it soft. "Don't worry. All we want is a very descriptive story on how you escaped the Thunderbirds. What were their names—Fielderlow and Cacklefront?"

Maddix gulped.

"Yes, I'm sure you know them," Jackelhide said. "And it would be *such a shame* to see people get hurt, would it not?"

Maddix gulped again. So it was the Thunderbirds thing they wanted. *What is it with the whole 'story in full detail' and 'descriptive story' thing?* Maddix wondered.

"I... I'm not gonna tell you," he said, his voice as strong as it could be at this moment.

"Well, I know that you are very scared at the moment, with it being dark and all," Jackelhide said, "but listen to me: this can all be over if you give me a descriptive—and I mean *descriptive*—story on how you escaped Cacklefront and Fielderlow."

"What about Luke?" Maddix asked. "And Nicole?"

"Them?" Jackelhide said. "Oh, they'll be fine. Unless—" he called to the others. "Ready the other victims!" and he turned back to Maddix. "—they won't be."

Maddix knew lives could be at stake. What if he kept resisting, and the manticores tortured Nicole and Luke? And, for all he knew, Luke could already be dead!

No, he told himself firmly, *don't think that. Luke's not dead. I would feel it.* It was kind of stupid to convince himself that he could feel it if his best friend died, but he just knew that he would. And who was he to claim this was a life-or-death situation, anyway?

"What will happen to them if I don't tell you what I know?" Maddix asked Jackelhide.

He laughed. "Answers for answers, boy. I'll tell you what I know after—and only after—you tell me what you know. It's just how life works."

"No," Maddix said, suddenly angry. "That's not how it works." Judging by Jackelhide's tone now, Maddix imagined him grinning, but trying not to.

"You know," he said, nearing closer to Maddix, "one of your friends might be as near as right next to you. You just don't realize it." Maddix almost called out, "Nicole? Luke!" to the darkness, but then he realized that Jackelhide was playing mind games with him.

Well, Maddix thought, *better fight fire with fire.*

"And maybe one of your kind is a double-crosser," Maddix said, standing so close to Jackelhide that he could smell his breath, "and you don't know it yet." He sensed that Jackelhide had looked around at the others for a split-second—but a split second was only a split second.

Jackelhide laughed again. "Didn't I tell you not to play games with me, Parker? Are you really as dumb as you look?"

Maddix was very offended. "And are you really as loyal to your master as you should be?"

"What?" Jackelhide seemed very surprised to even be asked this question. "What do you mean? I am his top servant, higher than any other—"

"Higher than Zennith?" Maddix asked. He could tell just by Jackelhide's voice that all the color had drained from his face. "You know about Zennith?" he gasped.

"Of course I do," Maddix said, remembering his first conversation he had with him. He also saw the control he had here. "And I also know that you are not in the same rank as him. Poor you, with a life that is *never* fulfilling."

"What—I—no!" he managed to say. "What do *you* know about *my* life?"

"All sorts of things," when Maddix said this, he was sure that Jackelhide had been thinking, *Why'd I ask that, why'd I ask that?*

Think—that's it! He could use his powers! *Wait,* Maddix thought, *Jackelhide said that he and the other manticores had their minds blocked and impenetrable.* That sure was a problem.

Hey, he suddenly thought, *who am I to listen to a monster who thinks he can trick me and boss me around? For all I know, he could be lying! Let's go find out.*

He fixed a gaze right into where he hoped (and hoped and hoped and hoped) that Jackelhide's eyes were. In fact, his gaze was so strong, Maddix thought that whoever got this look had the impression that they were about to Dislike What was About to Happen.

"Hey, kid, what are you doing?" came Jackelhide's worried voice. "You're not talking…" Then he put the pieces together. "Hey, my mind's blocked, so don't you try—"

But it was too late.

Maddix suddenly saw a whole mind-full of letters and numbers spread out in front of him. Knowing he only had a few seconds, he searched frantically for a piece of information that would help him escape the manticore's clutches. Finally, he found it. There it was, plain as day: *Don't let him see your weakness, which is—*

But it was too late. Before he knew what was happening, he was soaring back to the darkness, Jackelhide in front of him.

"What's the matter?" the manticore's sneer was back. "Did it not work?"

"It—worked," Maddix said. *I don't get it,* he thought, very scared, *why was my time so short? What am I gonna do now? Jackelhide knows I'm trying to use my powers...*

"So, do you have any weapons to fight me with? Any *powerful words of wisdom* you saw? Powers you can wield? Thoughts you can use against me?" Jackelhide became so annoyingly malicious that Maddix seriously considered covering his ears.

"And I don't even know," he went on, "why the routine is going on. You getting into a spot of trouble, then getting out of it, you getting into a spot of trouble, then getting out of it, you getting into a spot of trouble, then getting out of it—you know, it's really repetitive. And I'm gonna change that." Maddix realized: there *was* a pattern. And he would keep it going.

"Are—are you sure?" Maddix asked.

"Yes," Jackelhide said, "and you are not going to get any more attempts to stop me."

"Why?" the word was out of his mouth before Maddix could stop it.

"Because you'll be with your friend," Jackelhide said.

Maddix barely had time to wonder what on earth he was talking about before he was falling again.

CHAPTER 31
THE PING-PONG GAME

P rotect, don't protect, protect, don't protect..."

"You're really into this, aren't you, Zennith?"

Zennith paused to look up at Sidero. "Who, me? Uh—yeah, I was watching this."

Sidero bit back a laugh. "Yeah, Parker's done pretty well keeping himself intact."

"What do you mean?" Zennith asked, tearing his gaze away from the darkness.

"Jackelhide sounds like he wants to tear him limb from limb," Sidero said, smiling. "Don't you hear him? That 'are you really as dumb as you look?' and the 'are you really as loyal to your master as you should be?' thing is really getting them good."

"It's like a ping-pong game," Zennith said enthusiastically. "Exchanging remarks, left, right, left, right, left, right..."

"And Parker's got it clean, taking the swipe with the 'Higher than Zennith' attack," Zennith said, like a commentator at a championship game. "Who knows how he thought to use that move, folks, got Jackelhide in shock. And right on time, too, gives him time to dodge the manticore's next blow. In fact, ladies and gentlemen, he is fighting back against Parker's remark. How do you know about my life, people, that's it right there. And Parker's going in for the slam again with a burn so hot it could melt the beast's hind legs off; He is using his powers! Repeat: *he is using his powers!* Someone get me a microphone, he is going loud and proud!"

Sidero laughed. "Yes, he is advancing, then retreating, advancing, retreating, everyone watching his moves!"

"You know, this is the most fun we've had in eleven years," Zennith said, smiling. "The evil forces have been lying low, encouraging the occasional burglary, but nothing else."

"Yes, it's been sad," Sidero said, shaking his head. "All of our talents and allies being put to waste."

"Wait a second," Zennith put out a hand. "What's Jackelhide doing? I wish we could see."

"Put this on," Sidero said, handing him a pair of goggles. "Night vision."

"Why didn't you give me these before?" Zennith asked, but Sidero said, "Never mind that. Turn the dial and listen."

Zennith spun the dial and strained his ears. He saw Parker, looking around with a panicked expression.

"Wait—is he falling *again*? Geez, that kid's seen more rushing air than I have—and I've been skydiving."

"He pretty much is, they way he's falling," Sidero said, using his own goggles. "There's just no parachute."

"Wait, did Jackelhide say something about 'joining your friend?' Oh, I know what he's doing! The Wizard of Oz Method." Zennith said.

"What's that?" Sidero asked, turning to look at him.

"It's where Jackelhide uses magic to make Parker believe Vincent's with him, but it's just a—"

"Hologram," Sidero said. The two beings looked at each other—and laughed.

CHAPTER 32
THE WIZARD OF OZ METHOD

Maddix wondered where on earth Nicole was. And Luke. Were they being held prisoner? Were they already dead? *No,* he thought firmly, *we talked about this—they're not dead!* A little voice in his head whispered, *Just keep saying it till you believe it. What do you know?*

A lot of things, he said to it, and I also know that they're alive and I should fight whatever I have to so I can get to them.

Don't get too cocky, the voice said, *your Electro Pencil doesn't work, you're powerless.*

Not quite, Maddix said, I've got my powers.

Not so fast, the voice sneered, *your powers are glitching, remember?*

Right. There was that problem.

Maddix looked around; this was his third time falling, right? *Wow,* he thought, laughing slightly, *Sidero sure does like to keep me in the air.* Now that he was thinking about Sidero, he wondered what the villain looked like. Was he an animal? A man? Maddix remembered when he'd first entered Zennith's mind, he'd seen Zennish shaking hands with a hooded figure. He remembered the pain in his chest when he first saw it. *Evil.* Most definitely evil.

The world was dark, the wind whistling in his ears, and Maddix just waited, wondering when he would stop falling. He'd been through this so many times that he just thought it was getting old.

Suddenly, there was a voice. Maddix whirled around, eyes alert. But then he realized the voice didn't belong to Jackelhide. It belonged to someone else.

"Maddix! Hey, Maddix! Over here!"

Maddix couldn't believe it. The voice he heard was one of his favorites. And, the voice was one of those he desperately wanted to hear.

"Luke!"

His voice was distant, but it was there. Maddix asked, "Where are you?"

"Over here!"

Maddix edged towards his voice. Finally, his outstretched arms found something.

"Luke, are you there?" he asked.

The voice was practically screaming in his ear. "Yeah, can't you feel me?"

After having dealt with Cacklefront in Nicole's room, he felt so sure that it was Luke that he didn't bother checking if it was his best friend or not.

"Where have you been?"

"I was in the East tower, like Nicole's dad a couple months ago," he explained. "I was bound, gagged, and I couldn't move. Then, after what seemed like hours, a strange man in black clothes came in and said, 'Darkness, Vincent.' And he pushed some button in his hand, and I was falling."

Maddix thought. "Why'd he say 'Darkness, Vincent?' Did he say anything about 'joining your friend?'"

"No," Luke said, "that's all he said. In the span of two seconds, when he said that and when he pushed the button, I wondered what he meant. So, of course, I didn't have much time to think."

Maddix narrowed his eyes. Luke didn't talk like this. He didn't take the time to choose his words so carefully that they blended with the others. There was something weird going on...

"Luke, did you see Jackelhide? Or the other manticores?" he asked.

"Manticores?" Luke sounded surprised. "There are manticores *here*? Are Thunderbirds here, too? What about Cacklefront and Fielderlow? They were the ones that captured me in the first place!"

That's pretty reasonable, Maddix thought, *Cacklefront and Fielderlow probably* did *capture Luke, but what about the manticores? Has he been in here long enough to know about them? This isn't right...*

"So, do you have a plan?" Luke asked.

"What plan?" Maddix said, puzzled.

"The one to get out of here?" Luke said.

"Oh," Maddix said, "well, first we have to get Nicole..."

There was a *smack!* Maddix guessed Luke had just slapped himself on the forehead. "That's right—Nicole! I forgot about her for a second! Do you have any idea where she is?"

"Nope," Maddix shook his head. "Do you?"

"Well, not really," Luke replied, "I just think that we should—"

Suddenly, Maddix thought—*wait, I could use my powers!* and he asked Luke, "Hey—where are you standing?"

"Why?" Luke asked.

"I—just want to know where you are," Maddix lied. He tried to act casual as he said, "Do you have a candle— or a lantern—by chance? I'm just so used to the dark."

"Um, I have a flashlight in my pocket," Luke said. He pulled it out. "Do you want it?"

"Yeah," Maddix said, reaching. "Can I?"

"Come over to me," Luke said. "I'll give it to you."

Now Maddix was *sure* that this wasn't Luke; he never was prepared anything, so he couldn't have brought a flashlight.

"Come here," Luke said. Maddix came closer to him, and felt a *thud!* on his head, and the world went black.

CHAPTER 33
SIDELINES

He knocked him out! I can't believe it, *he knocked him out!*"

"Yes, yes, it's beyond hilarious," Sidero rolled his eyes.

"Stop it, it was funny!" Zennith exclaimed. "He's like, 'come here, I'll give it to you,' and then he's like, 'okay, sure,' and then he bangs him on the head with it and *knocks him out!*"

"Shh, you might get us heard," Sidero whispered, "and judging by your tone, Parker probably already has."

"Fine," Zennith said, "it was just hilarious, though! He didn't suspect a thing."

"I think he did," Sidero said, "when he said, 'I just— want to know where you are,' he sounded like he knew what was up."

"I guess," Zennith shrugged. "I just wish we could watch it on replay."

Sidero rolled his eyes again.

"Kidding," Zennith smiled. "So, what should we do with him now?"

"That's the tricky part," Sidero said, "we can't keep him here, or he'll wonder where his friend is. And we can't take him back to Apollo, since he'll think he got away, so all we have left is—"

"Take him somewhere he isn't familiar with," Zennith finished the sentence for him. "But where?"

"And we need that someplace to be maddening," Sidero said. "You know, to confuse him."

"Yes," Zennith nodded. "What if we—" Sidero cut him off.

"No, no, no. Whatever you are going to say, I have a better idea." He whispered something in his ear.

"Brilliant," Zennith said. "That room like an Escape Room?"

"I told you," Sidero said, nodding. He looked back at the darkness. "That boy's as good as gone."

CHAPTER 34
THE FIRECATCHER

Maddix opened his eyes and groaned. He felt his head. It hurt. *A lot.* Was that a flashlight? *Whatever it was,* he thought, *it was heavy.* He almost blacked out again just thinking about it. He looked around. *Where am I?*

The walls were blank, a maddening white. The floor was white as well, and the ceiling light above was reflecting off it. All that white was driving him crazy.

"Hello?" he said. "Is anyone here?" He spotted a door, and struggled to get up. With difficulty, he managed to get on his feet and walk toward it. Maddix reached for the doorknob, but it disappeared before he could touch it. Then, the whole door vanished, and other ones appeared all around the room. Door after door after door after door—there was no end. Whenever Maddix inched towards one, it disappeared without a trace.

He'd seen something like this before. When they were younger, Luke had played a game with a white room like this on his dad's computer. It was called the Escape Room. Was he supposed to escape? *Well, duh,* he thought, *but how? This room's so—blank.*

There was a red piece of paper on the floor. Maddix tentatively walked towards it and cautiously picked it up.

Then, there was wind—huge, strong wind—and Maddix covered his face with the hand that wasn't holding the red paper. And the fire—there was fire—it was coming from all the walls. Maddix looked down at the red paper and he saw himself. It was a shiny glass, reflecting back at him! But that didn't seem to matter at that moment. The air was smoke, and Maddix coughed. The smoke was thick, and he couldn't take it. He fell down and the fire came nearer. The heat of the fire clouded his brain, his very thoughts. He felt his blood pumping in his head, his heartbeat quickening. Over the sound of the his beating heart, he heard a smash: the glass shattered in his hands.

Help, he thought desperately, *help, somebody—anybody...*

Suddenly, there was a whooshing sound—and the fire rushed towards him. Instinctively, he held out both of his hands to shield himself, and he closed his eyes, waiting for the pain to come. But—there was nothing. He opened his eyes and looked at his hands. He gasped: he was *holding the fire.*

It was curled in circles, and Maddix directed it at the walls, blank and white. The tangible fire he saw in his hands matched the fire-like feeling he felt in his heart in a way he couldn't explain. He fired, and the flames lauched from his hand hit the wall, scorching them. He brought his hands back in a pulling motion, and the scorch marks collected again and formed fire. He fired again, and again, until the wall broke.

Maddix saw another room, charcoal black this time, and stepped into it. On a podium in the middle of the room was a grappling hook. It was one of those grappling hooks that someone could launch towards someplace high, and it would pull them up. *Why's there a grappling hook here?* He wondered. He shrugged, looked around, and took it. He launched it towards the ceiling, and it brought him up towards the chandelier. He felt like a spy robbing a museum. *Well*, he thought, *this museum's weirder than most of them.*

Maddix thought back to all the spy movies he'd ever watched. He sighed: the number added up to zero. How was he going to get out of here? So far, he'd only gotten here on instinct and the feeling of somehow knowing what to do. Now, however, he was suspended in midair, exposed to anyone who wished to enter.

Maddix thought of Sidero—the most evil being in the world—who could walk in and end his life. It brought shivers down his spine. *No,* he thought, *Sidero himself wouldn't do me in. He would probably send his servants—*

Zennith, perhaps, or more monsters— but never himself. He sure would risk a lot, waltzing into a room where a helpless boy—emphasizing the word helpless—hung down from the chandelier. Yes, he would risk so much, I could destroy him in one hit.

Maddix shook his head. *I need a plan*, he told himself, *there's no time to get sarcastic, and it won't help, either. Study your surroundings, be in the moment.* He looked around. The room was just plain black, with the single podium in the center, and the glimmering chandelier from which he was hanging. It looked about twenty or thirty feet off the ground.

The chandelier was right in the middle of the ceiling, so he couldn't leap over to the walls. And all he had was a grappling hook. A stupid grappling hook. He tested his fire again and propelled flames to the opposite wall, charring them. So, he thought, he still had a way to defend himself if anyone else came in.

Suddenly, Maddix heard footsteps. He looked around frantically, wondering where he could hide. He looked down at his clothes—*black*. The same color as the ceiling. *Oh, thank—* he didn't have time to finish his thought as two men in hoods walked in, and he climbed to the top part of the chandelier. Maddix held his breath as it made noise, but it seemed that the men were too busy talking to notice.

"It was just a classic Aladdin case," the first man said. Maddix noticed his voice was slightly familiar. Where had he heard it before?

"I know," the other man said. His voice wasn't familiar at all. In fact, Maddix never would've guessed a man could have such a voice. But then again, was he a man? "But he's highly dangerous now, you know that. We're handing him weapons, and we barely have enough for ourselves!"

"Calm yourself," the first man said. "At least we know what 'shattering the glass' means, so we don't have as many questions as before—"

"No, that is incorrect," the second man said, "we have more questions now, way more than I could've ever dreamed!"

"But surely—this isn't our fault?" the first man asked, worry in his tone.

"I have to say it is," the second man sighed. "And he could be in this room right now!"

"Yes, yes, I know," the first man said. He scanned the room. "But, is there a way he—*couldn't*—be here? Because if he is, he is hiding himself very well. And that's a problem for us."

"Well, if he *is* here," the second man told the first, "we need a way to get him to come out of hiding."
"I agree, but how?" the first man asked.

"I know the perfect way," the second man said, "follow my lead, Zennith."

"Of course," Zennith replied, "of course, Sidero."

They lowered their hoods.

Maddix screamed.

And he fell.

CHAPTER 35
KID IN BLACK

The crashing noise was deafening, and Sidero and Zennith looked down. The kid was sprawled on the floor, grappling hook in hand. Zennith took it.

"I've been looking for this," he said.

Sidero wasn't listening. He was too busy pulling up his hood. He'd known that it would lead them right to Parker. He just didn't realize it was that easy.

Zennith looked at Sidero, his expression saying, "What should we do?"

Sidero whispered, "I think he's blacked out again, because of how high he was. We shouldn't have a problem right now." Zennith still stepped back.

"What are you so scared about?" Sidero asked him. "He's an eleven-year-old kid!"

"I know," Zennith said, still stepping back. He pointed to the walls. "But look—scorch marks. Do you think..."

Sidero looked over, and seemed to know what Zennith was thinking.

He started laughing.

"What, you think he's a *Firecatcher?*" he asked. "Zennith, if I didn't know better, I'd say *you'd* just hit the ground hard. I mean, I know Firecatchers run in families, but someone's got to teach it to you in order for your powers to be harnessed. Parker was one when his father died—he couldn't have taught him. And, we haven't had a Firecatcher in—"

"Ten years." Zennith said. "And there haven't been any Firecatchers since, so they must all be gone."

Sidero said, "Right. His father was the last Firecatcher, and didn't have time to teach him."

"Right," Zennith said. "It's been ten years since you sent me to his house to take the last Firecatcher's powers. But I..." He mumbled something indistinct.

"Huh? What was that, Zennith?" Sidero grinned. "I can't quite hear you."

Zennith took a deep breath. "I made a mistake."

"Right you did," Sidero nodded solemnly. "And then you saw the mother and thought she had the powers, too."

"And she did!" Zennith said defensively. "She—kind of! She kind of did!"

"Yes, she was in training," Sidero nodded. "You remember you can be trained by someone who has the powers?"

"Yes," Zennith said. "So I used my magic correctly and took what little powers she had. She had laser eyes, too, She had to be dealt with."

"You used your magic correctly?" Sidero asked.

Zennith wrung his hands together. "Well, maybe not *correctly...*"

"Go on," Sidero was amused now.

"So when I found him," Zennith said, indicating the boy lying on the floor, "I couldn't just leave him."

They paused, and looked at Maddix laying motionless for several moments.

The boy stirred, and Zennith said, "How much longer?"

"An hour or so," Sidero replied. "That gives us enough time to do... whatever we're going to do."

"I'm glad," Zennith nodded. "He can get a little— defensive, when he knows what's happening."

Sidero studied Zennith. "You think so?" he asked. "You think when he knows what's happening, he fights for himself? Explain."

"With the Thunderbirds," Zennith told him, "when he figured out their intentions, he decided to use his powers to defend himself. And with Lucian, as soon as he figured out he wanted information from him, he told him he wouldn't talk. And with the manticores, he figured out that they wanted a detailed story from him, and he risked using his powers. Of course, they didn't work, but he was still trying to defend himself."

"Speaking of that, why *didn't* his powers work?" Zennith asked.

"Parker was under a lot of pressure," Sidero explained, "and he had doubt that it would work. So, his mind was clouded and his powers could only work for about five or six seconds. And Jackelhide knew it, too."

"Interesting," Zennith said, nodding. He looked back at the boy. "I suppose we should take all of his powers now."

"No," Sidero said, "let's see what he does with them."

CHAPTER 36
THE TRUTH HURTS (SO MUCH)

Maddix opened his eyes, and the first thing that went through his mind was the memory of him falling from a chandelier at the feet of two villains. He was about to yell, "Help! Somebody help me!" But he didn't. He gripped his head. It hurt more than when the fake Luke had knocked him out with the flashlight. How long had he been out? Half an hour? An hour?

It took him a moment to realize he was looking at blackness. Something felt soft on his face. He tried to bring his arms up, to feel it. But, he couldn't move his hands. He asked, "Hello?" but his voice was strangely muffled. He was kneeling, and the walls around him were very hard. He found that out when someone forced his hand out of its binding and slammed it onto the wall.

"Cold hard stone," the voice said. "You've got it good, Parker." Maddix knew that voice: Zennith, servant to Sidero. He fought back a groan.

Maddix wanted to say, "Where am I?" but then he remembered: he was gagged. He wiggled around, and it fell from his mouth. He quickly asked where he was before Zennith could put it back in.

"You never left where you came in," Zennith replied. "You're still here—except the circumstances are a little *different*."

Maddix wondered how. He sniffed. The air was the same as in the Black Room when he'd first seen Sidero and Zennith enter. How could the circumstances be different? And were they more dangerous now? *Stop kidding yourself*, a voice in his head said, *of course it's one hundred times more dangerous. What you really need to do is rip that blindfold off.*

Well, if you haven't noticed, Maddix told it, I'm kind of TIED TO THE WALL HERE!

Sheesh, the voice said, *calm down and think of a plan. Can your powers still work?*

I don't know, Maddix said to it, they didn't work for Jackelhide. Maybe I shouldn't use them anymore...

Are you crazy? Your powers have saved your life a million times! Use them or you die.

Fair point, Maddix replied, I'll try it. But I need to find out where Zennith's eyes are.

Hmmm, the voice responded, *that's hard. Oh! Just have him keep talking, and do the DWAH face towards his voice!*

Wouldn't I do it towards his whole face, then?

Stop asking stupid questions, go do it!

Maddix tried to do something to make Zennith talk (he still had the gag in) and he finally seemed to notice after a minute of awkward squirming.

"What're you doing, there?" he asked. *There.* Maddix did the DWAH face right at Zennith's voice.

"Oh, c—" He didn't hear the rest of Zennith's words, for he saw fire and was in his mind.

He saw the familiar landscape of letters and numbers, and then he saw something different. A hand, a huge hand, was coming towards him. Something told Maddix it wasn't a memory. The hand made the "OK" sign, and then brought its pointer finger up really fast—and it *flicked him.*

Maddix was falling, and he landed with a hard *thud!* back towards the stone wall.

"That's too bad," Zennith said. "Guess your powers don't work here." Maddix closed his eyes, and took a deep breath. He had to be calm here.

That's right, the voice in his head said, *now try again. I promise it'll work this time.*

Maddix remembered where Zennith was and shot him the DWAH face. He entered his mind again and saw what he was looking for: *Keep him from calming himself down; his powers don't work when he's under pressure. Make sure he doesn't calm himself down...*

So *that's* why his powers hadn't worked with Jackelhide! Maddix found something else that caught his eye.

I can't believe Parker's father was the last Firecatcher! Shame he died...it wasn't nearly my fault... And his mother...well, she's dead presumably, she was never found in the ashes of the house...

For a moment, Maddix forgot what he was doing, that he was bound and gagged and trying to fight an evil villain. All he remembered were the words echoing in his brain—*he died, it wasn't nearly my fault...His mother, she's dead presumably, she was never found...*

So his parents were dead. The cold, hard truth hit him like a wrecking ball to a building.

He was back at Zennith's feet—and the worst part was that Sidero's servant knew what he'd seen.

"So, you found out, didn't you?" he asked. "Well, now that you're learning stuff..."

He took the blindfold off.

Maddix looked down.

He screamed again.

CHAPTER 37
AGAINST ~~THE WALLS~~ SOMETHING MORE DANGEROUS THAN WALLS

Zennith had to play the "Mean and Threatening Villain" role to the kid, and he wasn't doing too well at it. He thought he was doing okay until Parker went into his mind the second time.

Judging by his haunting silence, the shocked silence, he must've seen his thoughts on his parents. Zennith kind of felt sorry for him, to finally discover the truth when you're in the clutches of a villain. And when you're dangling right underneath a much more powerful villain—the *most powerful* villain, at that.

So there he was, Maddix Parker, dangling from the chandelier, with the most feared enchanter in the world on top of it. Zennith knew this would freak him out a lot, which is why he and Sidero decided to do it. Sidero was looking down at him, hand held up.

Sure enough, Zennith saw the boy's fearful eyes look up at him, but Maddix's tone was strong as he said, "You think that scares me?"

Zennith almost laughed out loud. "Yes, I think that *does* scare you," he said.

"Why should I be scared?" Maddix asked.

"Because," Zennith looked at Sidero, "he can do this."

Sidero clapped—a huge clap, like thunder—and a large ball of ice ricocheted off the walls and right to him. He ducked; and the ice ball hit the wall behind him.

"Scared now?"

CHAPTER 38
ICE AND BURN

Maddix knew very well that Zennith knew he was scared, but he still could deny it. And of course Sidero's ice scared him—it scared him *to death*—but he wasn't about to show that to Zennith. When Zennith asked again if it scared him, he just shook his head. Zennith didn't seem dismayed.

Sidero shook the whole room, and then looked at Maddix, smirking. Maddix closed his eyes. *This isn't happening, this isn't happening...*

Unfortunately, it *was* happening.

Sidero used his powers to shake his cable, so he swung back and forth. Maddix was starting to get dizzy.

"I've got powers too!" he shouted. "And—and if you don't stop right now, I'll unleash them!"

"Oh, you figured out that you're a Firecatcher and now you think that can save you?" Sidero said mockingly.

"Or you'll go into my mind? Come on, kid, it won't work."

"Oh really?" Maddix said. "How can you be so sure?"

"Let's see here," Zennith said, "you're hanging in midair, no experience whatsoever, and we're watching you, with all the power and experience one can have."

Maddix frowned. He was right. Zennith was hanging from a cable right next to him, and Maddix didn't have experience. Well, he kind of did, but not with the *most feared enchanter in the world.* And he was unarmed, except for him being a—Firecatcher, was it? Seems about right— and having the power to go into someone's mind.

He could try Zennith's again. Now that he could see, he could properly do the DWAH face and enter his mind. All he had to do was stay calm.

He looked at Zennith, right into his eyes. He made the DWAH face, and—

SMASH!

Maddix slammed against the (solid stone) wall again and swung back. He saw a lot of men in black suits with hoods burst through the door. They were each holding silver discs. One threw a disc at Sidero, who had to jump from his cable to avoid it, and he was instantly grabbed by another one as he reached the ground. The other suited man grabbed Zennith.

One man threw a disc at Maddix's cable and it zinged through the air, and broke the cable. Maddix went sprawling to the floor. Luckily, it wasn't as high as when he'd used the grappling hook. Another man pointed the disc at him and he said quickly, "No, no, you don't understand—"

The man lifted his hood and Maddix gasped.

"*Mr. Vincent?*"

CHAPTER 39
CLOCKWISE

The men grabbed hold of Sidero and Zennith, and carried them towards the far wall. The two villains nodded at each other, and there was a rush of wind as they vanished. They reappeared in an abandoned tall, brick, building at the edge of a cliff.

"Embarrassing," observed Sidero, dryly.

"Yes, quite," Zennith said, taking his cloak off and hanging it over a chair. "The Magical Protection Force always gets in the way."

"Exactly," Sidero said, taking his gloves off, "and that is why the OGM will be the first to go when we take over the world."

Zennith nodded distractedly. He was looking fixedly at the table.

"What are you staring at?" Sidero asked him.

"Nothing," Zennith replied, looking up. "I'm just— thinking. About the time."

"The time?" Sidero said, walking over to him. "Why on earth would you be thinking about the time?"

"It's running out," Zennith responded. "Even the clock knows it. You see: it's going faster. Look." He pointed to the wallclock. To one's eye, it looked like the hour and minute hands were speeding up. But it could've just been an illusion. After all, they'd been thinking about the time a lot lately.

"When does Parker turn twelve again?" Zennith asked, not taking his eyes off the clock.

"November thirtieth," Sidero replied. "What day is it again?"

"November third," Zennith said.

"We've got twenty-seven days to stop him," Sidero said hoarsely. "Or he wins."

"And he's already done something, too," Zennith whispered. "He's shattered the glass already."

"There's no way to stop him from turning twelve," Sidero said, "but there is a way to stop him from interfering with us. Where's the Rader girl, and the real Vincent boy?"

"Uh, Rader's with Jackelhide," Zennith said, looking at his computer, "and Vincent's in the North tower."

"Good," Sidero said, speaking like a businessman. "Tell Jackelhide to throw Rader to Parker. *Throw her*—literally *throw her*—and send Vincent crashing through the walls to his room."

"Why?" Zennith asked. "That sounds like they're going to get killed!"

"They won't," Sidero said, "they'll just be in pain for a couple of weeks. They won't even pass out."

Zennith looked at him.

"What?" Sidero said, then he went back to business. "Make sure Jackelhide, the manticores, Thunderbirds, serpents, griffins, *no one*, interferes with them. Make it look like we've forgotten all about them."

"Okay," Zennith replied. "Do you think it will work?"

"Definitely," Sidero answered. "Parker is brave enough to hold back his fear even when he's in the same room as me, but he's basically helpless when it comes to his friends being in danger."

"Perfect," Zennith said. He clapped his hands. "Game on."

CHAPTER 40
THROW-IN

Mr. Vincent smiled at Maddix, just after removing his hood. "What's up?"

"What's up?" Maddix repeated. "What's up? A lot of things!"

Mr. Vincent looked at him.

"Sorry," Maddix said. "It's just—took a lot of blows to the head today." Mr. Vincent smiled again.

"Come on," he said. "Let's get back to Apollo."

He gripped Maddix's hand and there was a great gust of wind. It took a moment for Maddix to realize *he was flying*.

"How is this happening?" he asked.

"Powers," Mr. Vincent replied. He winked at him.

A second later, they were standing at Apollo's doors. Maddix ran up to the safety of his and Luke's bedroom, and flopped down on his bed. What had *happened* in the last few hours? *Hmm, let's see*, he thought, *I became a*

Firecatcher, I realized my dad was a Firecatcher, I found out my parents are dead, I figured out how they were killed, and I almost got killed myself about five times.

That was a lot to handle.

Maddix sat up. He almost forgot about Luke and Nicole! Where were they? And the manticores. Jackelhide must have them! Maddix went to Mr. Vincent's office and asked him if he knew where they are.

"Sorry Maddix," he said, "the Magical Protection Force is trying to locate them, but we've got no luck."

Maddix frowned. Then he realized something. "Wait, the Magical Protection Force? You're a part of it?"

"Yes," he replied, "I didn't know why you didn't ask before. So yes: I am in charge of Apollo Academy and I am also a member of the Magical Protection Force of the OGM."

Maddix remembered that name: the OGM. Nicole had said something about it. "*A law was passed in the Office of General Magic, or OGM, that each child showing magical activity should go to the Power Analyzation to be analyzed.*" She'd said that to him and Luke when she had been explaining about the Power Analyzation.

So the Magical Protection Force was part of the OGM. Maddix looked at Mr. Vincent. His best friend's dad was a part of the Office of General Magic?

"I'm not feeling so good," Maddix said, and he hurried back to his room before Mr. Vincent could ask anything else.

Not even two minutes later, there was a whirring noise and Maddix found himself being tackled by someone.

"Hey, get off me!"

Then, he realized that the person who had tackled him was a girl, with long blonde hair in a braid. Maddix's eyes went wide when he realized who he was seeing.

"Nicole!"

His friend stood up and noticed who she was standing next to.

"Maddix!"

Maddix asked, "Where've you been?"

"With the other manticores," she said, "not far from where you were, I could hear you and Jackelhide talking. I tried to call out to you, but the other manticores kept their claws over my mouth. And then I heard Luke's voice! Did you find him? Where is he?"

"Turns out," Maddix said, "it was another imposter of some kind."

He told her his story about the Firecatchers and what happened to him with Zennith and Sidero. When he'd finished, Nicole had her hand over her mouth.

"That's terrible!" she said.

"I know," Maddix nodded. "Do you know where the real Luke is?"

"No," Nicole shook her head.

There was another whirring sound, and Maddix hit the ground again. Nicole screamed. Then she gasped.

Maddix looked at the boy on top of him. He had sandy brown hair and blue eyes.

Maddix grinned.

"Luke!"

Luke looked up; he smiled broadly.

"Where've you been?" he asked.

Maddix laughed. "Where've *I* been? Oh, I don't know, fighting the scariest enchanter in the world!"

Luke's eyes went wide. "Seriously?" He looked at Nicole. "No. Seriously?"

Nicole nodded, speechless.

"Where were you?" Maddix asked.

"In the North Tower," Luke said.

"Wait here," Maddix ran to Nicole's room, picked something up, and ran back. "Did someone come in there in dark clothes? Did they say, 'darkness, Vincent'?"

"No," Luke said, confused.

Maddix shined the Truth Light on him. "Are you really Luke Vincent?"

"Yes," Luke answered.

Maddix turned it off. "Sorry," he said. "But last time, you were Cacklefront."

"What?" Luke looked totally lost. "What? Did—did I miss something?"

"You explain," Maddix said to Nicole.

Nicole rolled her eyes and explained everything from Cacklefront's most recent encounter with them to the manticores.

"…and then someone said, 'take the girl,' and someone took me away." Nicole finished. "And then I heard Maddix talking to one of the manticores—Jackelhide—and then…" She stopped, and tugged on her braid nervously. "I heard your voice."

"What?" Luke said.

"But that was another imposter," Maddix explained. "He knocked me out with a flashlight."

And then Maddix told him about the rest of it: the whole Firecatcher business, his encounter with Zennith and Sidero, and how Luke's own father had rescued him.

"Did *you* know he was part of the Magical Protection Force?" he asked.

"Well," Luke's brow was furrowed as he thought, "sometimes Dad says he has to go to work meetings. Remember, Maddix? Now I know what they were!"

"Yeah," Maddix nodded, remembering. "I mean, why do you have to *go somewhere* for a work meeting if you work at a school?"

"Um," Nicole began, but Luke held up a hand.

"Please," he said, "we don't need a lecture on what could happen in a school. Now, please—"

"Wait a second," Maddix went closer to him. "Luke, are you alright?"

"Yeah," Luke said quickly. "Of course I am. Never better. Never. Nope. Nada."

"He *does* look a little weary," Nicole said, walking next to Maddix and squinting. "Luke, were you tied up or something?"

"What?" Luke said. "No! What—tied up, are you guys crazy? If I had been tied up, I would've told you guys!"

"You were tied up, weren't you?" Maddix said, raising his eyebrow.

Luke sighed. "Okay, yes, and before you ask, it hurt— a *lot*. There you go."

"What do you mean?" Nicole asked. "Are you ashamed of it or something?"

Luke paused and looked at her.

She said, "Luke!"

"Luke, there's nothing wrong with it hurting!" Maddix said. "Is that what you were afraid of? That we would laugh or something?"

"Well, yeah," Luke shrugged. "I guess so."

"Come on," Maddix said, smiling. "We wouldn't laugh if you got pied in the face."

"Really?" Luke raised an eyebrow.

"Well, maybe," Maddix joked, "but not right now. Come on, let's figure out what's going on with Zennith and Sidero. Has the Magical Protection Force got them?"

"I doubt anyone would be able to hold them," Nicole said, "even the Magical Protection Force."

"Why don't we ask my dad?" Luke suggested. "I bet he knows all the goings-on."

They went to Mr. Vincent's office. Luke's dad jumped up at the sight of his son, and hugged him.

"Where in *the world* have you been?" he asked.

"The North Tower," Luke said, "but there's no time to explain now, Dad, we need to get answers."

"Okay," Mr. Vincent said. "Fire away."

"Has the Magical Protection Force still got Zennith and Sidero?" Maddix asked.

"No," Mr. Vincent turned to his computer and went to a website. "I got a report from one of the people who took them away. He says that they disappeared."

"They escaped?" Nicole said, her eyes wide.

"Yes," Mr. Vincent said again, scanning the report. "They vanished—*poof!*"

"Teleportation?" Luke said.

"A special teleportation," Nicole said, a smile tugging at the corners of her lips. "A kind of magic that is used when you have complete concentration on your destination and your brain wills you to go from one place to another. My dad told me all about it. It takes a bunch of practice and my dad said—"

"Okay, Nicole," Luke interjected. "We know they teleported." He turned back to his dad. "Go on."

"So, it looks like Zennith and Sidero are out of sight for awhile," Mr. Vincent said, not acknowledging his son's slight attitude. "Sorry, guys. And, even if we did have their location or we had them, I couldn't tell you. It's classified information."

"But we can handle stuff like that!" Luke said, puffing his chest out indignantly. "Maddix took down two Thunderbirds single-handedly! And Zennith and Sidero themselves!"

"No, I didn't," Maddix began.

But Luke quickly interrupted, "And he did it *twice*! One time with Fielderlow and Cacklefront, and the other time with just Cacklefront! We can take on lots of things!"

"Listen, Luke," his father said, "I know you have overcome a lot of dangers, but you're still three eleven-year-old kids. And Maddix was *almost killed* when he faced Zennith and Sidero. If it weren't for the Magical Protection Force, he would've been destroyed."

Maddix nodded.

"There's that," Nicole said, "but after Maddix gets better, we can go track them down! We know a lot more than you think! But, if we're just *three eleven-year-old kids*, I guess we'll sit down and watch some paint dry. I mean, that's the meaning of life, isn't it?"

"And, for the record, Maddix is almost twelve," Luke added.

Maddix shrugged. "I'm sorry Mr. Vincent; they speak the truth."

Mr. Vincent looked at them. "But Maddix has to recover."

"From what?" Luke asked.

"He said he wasn't feeling too good," Mr. Vincent said, looking at Maddix.

"No, I didn't," Maddix lied.

Mr. Vincent looked at him.

Maddix groaned. "*After?*"

Mr. Vincent stared at the three of them, each wearing an almost identical hopeful look.

He sighed. "Alright."

They cheered.

"*But only after,*" Mr. Vincent said, "Maddix is better. He could've gotten a severe concussion—or worse."

"I think I *got* worse," Maddix said, rubbing his head. "This thing's dynamite."

Maddix, Luke, and Nicole went back to Maddix and Luke's room. Maddix sat on the bed while Luke and Nicole were working at his desk.

"Come on, guys," he said. "You must have *some* plan."

"We do," Luke said. He shrugged on his coat and Nicole buttoned up hers. They walked to the door.

"What—you're leaving?" Maddix said. "Just like that? Take me with you."

"Sorry," Nicole said, almost squeaking. "You heard what Luke's dad said. You... you have to get better before you go with us."

"No," Maddix corrected, "he said you can't *do anything* that had to do with Zennith and Sidero before I got better."

"Let us try," Luke said. "Please."

"Let me come with you," Maddix said.

"No," Luke said firmly. He placed his hands on Maddix's shoulders and forced him down onto his bed. "You need to get better."

"But, if we get caught, you can be our backup," Nicole said.

"So you think I'm backup?" Maddix said indignantly, sitting up. It was either the throbbing pain in his head, or the anger in his heart at Zennith and Sidero, but something was influencing his heated attitude.

Luke and Nicole stepped back.

"Are—are you okay?" Nicole asked tentatively.

"Uh—yeah," Maddix said, clearing his head. "I—sorry. Just, recent events have totally destroyed my temper."

"Okay," Luke nodded. "So—you're cool with us going?"

"Well, no," Maddix said. He frowned. "What are you going to do?"

"Um—we're just going to the computer room," Nicole said. "To check their location. We think we know where they are."

"Where?" Maddix asked.

"Oh," Luke said. He looked at Nicole.

"Luke, you can tell him," she told him.

"Yeah," Maddix agreed.

"We think Zennith and Sidero are somewhere in the area," Luke said. "We think that they are somewhere around here—you know, close to Apollo. And we're going to—"

"Ambush them?" Maddix said. "What are your weapons? What's your plan? How are you going to attack?"

Luke and Nicole looked at each other.

"Er—we haven't thought of that yet," Luke said. "But—we'll think of something on the way."

"On the way, huh," Maddix sat back. "That's a pretty bad idea, just saying."

"We know," Nicole said, her voice quiet.

"And what about Mr. Vincent?" Maddix asked. "He's professional, he would be of some help."

"Do you think he would let us?" Luke asked.

Maddix knew the answer to that. "Well, if you're going to go," he said, reaching into his pocket, "you better take this. You'll probably need it more than I do."

Luke and Nicole looked at it admiringly.

"Your Electro Pencil?" Nicole said. "We can't take this, Maddix."

"Yes, you can," Maddix told them, "and you should. What if you're trapped in a room? Just point this thing's tip up toward the ceiling and let its electric beams do the job of blowing it up."

"Alright," Luke put it in his jacket. "Anything else?"

"Yeah," Maddix said, grinning. "Let me prove to you I'm ready to come." He concentrated really hard on what he was doing, and closed his eyes. He opened his palms and let the power surge through him. Then, he opened his eyes and looked down.

"Fire?" Nicole and Luke said.

Luke and Nicole stepped back.

"That's dangerous," Nicole said faintly. "You're not gonna hit us, are you?"

Maddix raised an eyebrow. He laughed. "Would I?"

Luke and Nicole smiled.

"So, you think you're ready to come with us," Luke said.

"You know me so well," Maddix said. Luke turned to Nicole. "Do you know of anything that can check that I'm healthy enough?"

"Uh, I think so," Nicole replied, reaching into her bag. She pulled out a baton. "I completely forgot, I have a Checker Wand!"

"She has *everything*," Luke whispered to Maddix. Nicole pushed a button and scanned Maddix.

"Everything's good," she said. "Except his head; it might cause severe pain once or twice during the mission."

"But not *all* of it, right?" Maddix asked.

"Not all of it, I'm sure," Nicole said. "Just, be expecting it."

"Okay," Maddix said. "Now, come on, before Mr. Vincent sees."

"Luke," Nicole turned to him, "if you please."

"Of course," Luke said, smiling. "If everyone will grab my arm." They grabbed his wrists and as he turned invisible, they did too. They walked quietly out of the room and into the hallway. Silently, they crept to the computer room and Luke turned them visible again. He pulled up a screen that showed where he thought Zennith and Sidero were, and Nicole and Maddix nodded. He had showed them an abandoned place not too far from Apollo Academy, and since it was abandoned, and had a creepy vibe, he thought Zennith and Sidero were bound to be there.

"How are we going to go there?" Nicole asked. "Sorry—I just realized that."

"Didn't you say something earlier about teleportation?" Maddix said. "Something about willing your mind to take you someplace."

"Yes," Nicole said, "but I also said that you had to have permission from the OGM."

"Zennith and Sidero didn't," Luke pointed out.

"Well," Nicole said irritably, "Zennith and Sidero are the *bad guys*, aren't they? The *villains*, on the run from the law?" When Luke didn't reply, she nodded at him. "Simple thinking."

"Quiet down, guys," Maddix said. "Now, Nicole, do you have any idea how to do it with multiple people?"

"Well, there was something in the OGM's *Book of Laws* about thinking about where you want to go and holding their arm. It's like with what we did with Luke's invisibility. Oh—but we have to do this." She unbuttoned her coat and turned around in a circle with it. "It works better with a longer coat."

Maddix and Luke laughed. "It's hilarious," Luke said, "but I'll do it. Nicole, we'll grab your hand 'cause you sound like you know what you're doing." They clutched her arm and swished their coats... and they were gone.

CHAPTER 41
FIREWORKS

Zennith stepped to the door. He put his head on the wood and started thinking.

"What is it, Zennith?" Sidero entered.

"What are we going to do?" Zennith said, his head staying pressed against the door. "The clock is ticking, Parker's almost twelve, and we haven't heard from Lucian in weeks."

"I think you might want to rethink that last one," Sidero said, smiling. "Come check this out."

He led him through the back door and onto the cliffside. Zennith gasped as the sky was filled with bright lights.

"What is this?" he said hoarsely.

"Lucian," Sidero said simply.

"How—? Lucian? What?" Zennith was at a loss for words. "How do you know this is Lucian?"

"Our logo," Sidero pointed. "Whenever someone is sending us a message, or we are sending them one, we put our special signature. Because, of course, we can't put 'to Sidero and Zennith,' or else the person sending it would get caught."

"Yes, I know," Zennith nodded. "Where is the signature?"

"Near the top, there," Sidero showed him one of the lights in the sky. There was a circle with a line through it, and at the end of the line was a big S. It was like a cursive g whose curl at the bottom went into its circle and the end of the line crashed into the S. The S, of course, stood for Sidero.

"Ah," Zennith said, seeing it. "What is Lucian saying, then? Is everything going well?"

Sidero squinted. "Hmm," he said, pointing at the lights. "Well, the squiggles over there means that he's hiding, but those circles mean that he's near the target, and that straight line means the target is getting closer to us. Interesting." He looked back at an amazed Zennith and said, "So, Parker's with his friends again. That was part of the plan, wasn't it? To have him meet up with his friends, and then we wouldn't interfere with him so it looked like we've forgotten all about him. That was the plan. Did you alert Lucian?"

"Yes," Zennith replied. "But—but what about the other part of the message? About Parker being near us? How is that possible?"

"Yes," Sidero said, stroking his chin. "We're fairly close to Apollo, so maybe that's why they're so close to us. But maybe he's picked up our exact location, also."

"Well, it couldn't have been that easy for them to locate us," Zennith said. "We're pretty well hidden."

"Listen," Sidero said, "we need to take this *seriously*. You told me before that we're running out of time. When his birthday comes, we're doomed."

"I know, so you can stop saying that?" Zennith said. "Let's take some *action*."

"No," Sidero said firmly. "We just went over this: the plan was *not to interfere with Parker and his friends*, unless—and only *unless*—the circumstances are *dire*."

"Got it," Zennith said. "Back to the part about him being near us—maybe he knows where we are?"

"Yes," Sidero responded. "How would he know, though?"

"His friends are pretty smart," Zennith said. "Maybe they had access to computers and tracked our location."

"How would they get here?" Sidero wondered.

"Maybe they learned teleportation?" Zennith suggested.

"No, that's impossible," Sidero said. He started this while smiling. "It's not like we did it in front of him a bunch of times—" His eyes widened. So did Zennith's.

They ran back into the building.

CHAPTER 42
INEXPLICABLE

Maddix breathed in the salty air. He gasped as he looked down and saw a few bits of dirt fall down the cliffside. He drew his sneakers away from the edge and inched towards Luke and Nicole.

"Look at this place," he said.

"Shh," Nicole said, crouching down and touching the earth.

"How exactly do we find them?" Luke whispered.

"I don't know," Nicole said quietly. Luke made them invisible and they crept along the grass. Maddix readied both his fire and his mind-reading powers as their feet crunched along the dirt. Nicole had her fists clenched, and Luke's teeth were bared. *Luke and Nicole don't know what's coming*, Maddix thought suddenly, *they didn't see Zennith and Sidero. Well, they saw Zennith, but they didn't see Sidero and how much damage they could do when they were together. What am I going to do? Will they get scared at the last minute and surrender? Or will they still get scared and not do anything at all, and I not only have to do all the work but save them as well?*

This is dangerous stuff, he reminded himself. If they volunteered to do this, then they'll stick to it. They will.

All three of them jumped as a gust of wind swept through the air and sent chills down their spines. Maddix suddenly clutched his head. It was unbearable pain. He guessed that this was what Nicole had said would happen. *Well*, he thought as waves of pain crashed down on him, *at least it's not during a fight.*

They walked on. After a few minutes, Maddix heard pounding. Was it his head again? He turned around as Luke pointed to the sky. He gasped; lights exploded in the dark blankness, with color and brightness that made him stare at it... and stare at it... and stare at it.

There was a circle, with a line through it. And an S at the end of that. That symbol was the biggest. There were other lights, too, sure—a bunch of squiggles and lines and other circles—but that symbol was the biggest. He wondered what it meant.

"What's that?" Luke asked.

"I don't know," Nicole said for the second time. *This really is the worst time for Nicole not to know things,* thought Maddix.

"Let—let's keep going," Luke said. Maddix could hear his teeth chattering. But it wasn't cold.

"Maddix," Nicole said. "Is your head hurting? Did it before?"

"Uh—it did before," Maddix said. "Why?"

"I was just wondering," Nicole shrugged. She turned away, and her eyes widened. "Whoa."

"'Whoa' what?" Maddix asked. He turned. He saw what was clearly 'whoa.'

There was a tall, brick building close to one of the edges of the cliff. Half of its windows were broken, the door was almost off its hinges, and the walls looked like they were barely holding up.

"Well," Luke said, "this looks like the place." He looked to Nicole. "Ladies first?" She threw him a dark look, and he backed up.

"Guess it's boys, then," he said. Maddix and Luke started toward it, and Nicole followed.

They were still invisible, so they could look through the windows. Maddix was first. He looked through the glass and saw a table, with two people sitting it. No, there was only one person. The other was more like a being. Maddix felt a sharp jab in his chest. He turned away, gasping.

"What is it, Maddix?" Nicole whispered. "What did you see?"

"Don't—look," Maddix said. He kept gasping, scared to death. He couldn't breathe. Sidero and Zennith were there. They were definitely there. Sitting at a table. Just like that.

223

It was scary.

Luke and Nicole looked confused. "What was in there?" Luke asked.

"Yeah," Nicole said. "Did you see Sidero and Zennith?"

Maddix nodded, at a loss for words.

"Did they look scary?" Luke asked.

"Don't be like that, Luke, of course they were scary," Nicole told him.

"You're right," Maddix said hoarsely. He didn't know why he was acting up now; he'd been right below Sidero before, and he'd *talked* to Zennith recently. Why did just *seeing* them make his head spin?

"Come on, let's go in," Luke said, stepping towards the door.

"Hold up," Nicole said, grabbing his hood. He stepped back.

"What?" he asked.

"We need a *plan*," Nicole said to him. "A P-L-A-N, so we don't *die*. D-I-E."

"Oh," Luke said. "Right. So, what do you have?"

"What do you mean?" she asked. "I don't have a plan. We said we'd think of it as we got here—"

"Which we forgot to do," Luke finished. "Oh."

Nicole turned to Maddix. "Do you have any ideas, Maddix?" she asked him. "You obviously know what Zennith and Sidero are like. What are their weaknesses?

What are they afraid of? Do you have *any* information about it at all?"

"Well," Maddix said. He thought back to what he realized with a shock had only been a few hours ago, when he had been hanging under Sidero, Zennith by his side. It had been one of the most scary situations in his life. "Well, I think—I, uh—I got nothing. All I really figured out was that I could only use my powers when I was calm—and that my dad was a Firecatcher, and how both of my parents died, of course. So there's that. Have you two got anything?"

Nicole's eyes widened. "Oh, Maddix, that must've been hard for you to find out," she said.

"I know, it's sad and we should really talk about this *later*," Maddix said quickly. "You know, when we're *not* risking our lives?"

"Right," Nicole said. "So, we have an Electro Pencil, mind-reading powers, fire, Super Hearing, and invisibility. What can we do with that?"

"Oh, I know!" Luke exclaimed. "What if I sneak over behind Zennith and Sidero, invisible, and Maddix goes into one of their minds and finds out some secret weaknesses, and we use them to take them down!"

"Or," Nicole said, "we could find out the secrets and go back to the *safety* of Apollo and tell the OGM all that they need to know about them."

"Wouldn't my dad know we went here, then?" Luke asked.

"We'll just make up a story," Nicole said.

"Alright," Maddix said. "Nicole, stay here and use your Super Hearing and see how it goes. If things go bad, improvise and *save us please.*"

"Got it," Nicole said. "If things go bad, I'll save you."

"Thank you," Maddix said.

"You gotten over *your fear* now?" Luke said to Maddix. "Ready to face Zennith and Sidero?" Maddix rolled his eyes.

Nicole made sure Zennith and Sidero were distracted—or at least fully engaged in their conversation—so Luke and Maddix could slip in through the door. Maddix held his breath as it made the slightest creak. Zennith and Sidero, miraculously, didn't look over. Maddix exhaled. Luke beckoned for him to keep going.

They crept behind Zennith, so Maddix had a clear view of Sidero's eyes. Careful to not breathe directly on Zennith, he made the DWAH face at Sidero. It took all of his willpower to do this, of course. Who would want to look into those terrible eyes? But, to his immense pleasure, he saw fire and faced the letters and numbers that were always in one's mind. He searched desperately for some chunk of information, while wondering why Sidero's mind looked like a normal human's. Then, he saw a difference: there was an image, floating all throughout the landscape. It was a circle, with a line through it. And at the end of it was an S. Maddix realized that this was the same image in the fireworks! What did it mean, though? *I've got no time to waste,* Maddix told himself, *keep searching.* After a couple more seconds, he found it: *What are we going to do? Parker's almost twelve, and he's already shattered the glass. We're running out of time. Lucian said he's close to him, but hiding. What help is that? And the Room of Secrets—we've got to keep the boy away from that room. He could learn the secrets of anything! And Zennith knows this very well...*

The Room of Secrets? What was that? *Well,* Maddix thought, *whatever it is, if Sidero doesn't want me in it, it must be important.*

And what was that whole thing about him being twelve, anyway? He was getting older, big deal. Were Zennith and Sidero just sad he had lived long enough to be twelve?

Then he saw another thought...

Evil is growing, its forces gaining, the power of the dark, and all things remaining. As the clouds block the sun, the dark blocks the light, and the bad and the good all resort to a fight. But when all is lost, when hope is diminished, evil will be done, over, finished. For the light in the dark has entered at last, a boy with the mind that shatters the glass. And as years pass, and the boy turns twelve, evil's last standing will never be held.

His thoughts continued, but they appeared faded to Maddix, like they were aged a long time.

Zennith didn't have to read the prophecy to me, I know it! But, he has a good point. And what IS 'shattering the glass?' Oh,

Zennith is right. It could be the act of breaking an intangible object, like hope or joy or friendship.

Friendship? As it processed in Maddix's brain, his chest burned again. Suddenly, he heard the voice in his head again. *Friendship?* it said. *You always knew you had something else in you. Sure, you're a Firecatcher, and you have mind-reading powers, but what's in your heart is faith. When you were always in trouble, did you have a doubt you would get out of it?*

Well…

You don't get it, it said, *your friends were always right there, by your side.*

Remember, Maddix reminded the voice in his head, they almost left without me.

Call it what you want, kid, they're still your friends. And they deserve that title.

So Sidero and Zennith had gotten it wrong—it wasn't *friendship,* really, it was faith.

Maddix felt himself soaring back to the present, Luke shaking him. His expression said, "Where have you *been?*"

Maddix shook his head. "You go back to Nicole," he mouthed. "Start running a little bit ahead. I'll catch up."

Luke gave him a worried look and mouthed, "Are you sure?" Maddix nodded. Luke turned, and as soon as he did, Maddix became visible. But not before he'd ducked under the table. Maddix didn't know why, but a sudden idea had come to him, something that really shouldn't have been satisfying, even though it was.

But it wasn't the smartest thing to do.

As Luke ran out the door, Maddix said into Zennith's ear, "Make sure you get the gist: Maddix Parker was here." Zennith whipped around; Sidero yelled.

Maddix bolted out the door and ran after Luke and Nicole. Luke was visible now, and he'd never seen him run so fast. Maddix streaked after them, and caught up with them after a couple seconds. Zennith and Sidero were tailing them, both firing their powers: Sidero made the same ice balls he had made before, and threw them with all his might at Maddix, Luke and Nicole. Zennith was trying to pull them back, using his powers, but not succeeding.

When they dared, Luke and Maddix clutched Nicole's hand, swished their coats, and focused their minds on Apollo's doors. But Sidero's hand looked like a claw as he fired his iceballs again, knocking the kids down. That thwarted their attempt at teleportation.

Maddix, Luke, and Nicole fell down, and the two villains caught up with them.

Zennith grabbed Maddix and Nicole, Sidero grabbed Luke. Zennith looked at Maddix.

"We've been waiting for you," he said.

CHAPTER 43
CAUGHT

Zennith heard a bumping noise, but he was too distracted. He was trying to think of a way to intimidate Maddix and his friends so that they never used their powers again.

He heard the breath first. Then the words. "Make sure you get the gist: Maddix Parker was here."

Sidero, who had been staring at the table, looked up. They stood up as the kid ran out of the room and outside. Zennith and Sidero ran after them. Parker and his friends were here! How could they have gotten here? How could they have found their location? But those questions were for later; now, it was time to catch them. Zennith and Sidero were using all the strength they could muster to catch at least one of them. But, they caught all three. As they stopped to teleport, Zennith and Sidero made one last attempt at catching them, and they succeeded.

"We've been waiting for you," he said to Parker.

Maddix didn't like it, and Zennith could tell. He started kicking like a madman, flailing his arms and legs, his friends following suit. Zennith yawned. He and Sidero brought them into the tall, brick building house. He heard the girl scream—Rader, was it? Zennith dropped Vincent and Sidero dropped Rader. Zennith pinned Parker against the wall.

"Don't move," Zennith said. "You know what we can do." Sidero guarded the other two.

"Now, listen," Zennith said. "We've had a little *problem* with you. You see that clock?" He pointed to the wallclock. "It's ticking. Tick, tock, tick, tock." He waved his finger and watched Parker's eyes follow it. "And do you know what happens to other people when the tick-tocking stops?" He stopped, for suspense. Then, he continued. "It could crush someone's hopes. Did you know that?" He crushed his finger with his other hand, holding Maddix to the wall with his elbow. Maddix shook his head.

"And when time gets to somebody," Zennith resumed, "their mind seems to fade away. Piece by piece." Maddix winced as Zennith pretended to flick something.

This is going to fun, Zennith thought maliciously.

CHAPTER 44
IN TROUBLE AGAIN

In truth, Zennith's words scared Maddix. He would even be honest: they scared him *a lot*. Like, "Please don't hit me cause I know you will" a lot. And he didn't know which was worse: when he was dangling under Sidero, Zennith right over to him, or being pinned against a wall with Sidero hanging over his two best friends. Yup, both scary.

Maddix saw on Zennith's face that he was having fun tormenting him. Maddix looked over his head; Nicole was staring at him, fear in her eyes. Luke's expression showed one word: "Oh." Maddix knew what Luke was thinking. He was realizing this was the evil Maddix had been up against. It was what had made his heart race, his head pound, and left him gasping for air.

Zennith saw Maddix looking at his friends. "Oh, them?" he said. "Well, we'll make a deal: you'll answer our questions with *full truth*, and we'll let them go. But if you don't…" Sidero picked them up. Nicole was in one hand, Luke in the other. Sidero smirked. Then, he dropped them. Nicole yelped as she hit the ground, startled but unharmed. (*Now that was unnecessary,* Maddix thought vaguely.)

"I think you know," Sidero said. Nicole almost shouted again. She hadn't heard Sidero speak to them. It was quite frightening at first.

"So, what will it be?" Zennith asked Maddix.

"Don't do it, Maddix!" Luke exclaimed.

"Quiet," Sidero said sharply.

"Yeah, don't do it!" Nicole squeaked, despite Sidero's maddening glare. Zennith turned back to Maddix. Maddix tried to think quickly. Of course, he couldn't answer their questions. And what *were* they, anyway? And if he did, would they keep their promise? And Zennith said they'd only let *Nicole and Luke* go—what about him? Detail was key.

"Come on, kid," Zennith said.

"Do—do I have time to think about it first?" Maddix croaked. Zennith noticed his fear. He smirked before saying, "Fine. You get five—let's say seven minutes to think about it. And you know what? You get you talk with your little friends before you make your decision." He tapped his watch, setting a timer. "Seven minutes— *go.*" He dropped Maddix and went over to Sidero. They went to a nearby corner and talked in hushed voices.

Pushing aside the suspicion of Zennith actually agreeing, Maddix quickly hurried over to Luke and Nicole.

"Maddix, I—" Nicole said.

"Don't," Maddix warned her. "We have no time. Quick, what should I do?"

"Well, you can't answer their questions, obviously," Luke said, "and you can't say no, or else we're goners."

"And what about their questions?" Maddix asked. "What will they ask?"

"Well, they'll probably ask for a story 'in full detail' about your escape from the Thunderbirds, and maybe the manticores, too," Nicole replied, "and other stuff."

"Try using your powers again?" Luke suggested. "And you can have fire reinforcements now! Use that!"

"And the Electro Pencil," Nicole handed it to him. He pocketed it. "Go unleash those electric beams on the ceiling." Maddix smiled.

He saw Zennith look over at him. And Zennith saw him looking at him, and he nodded. Zennith looked at his watch. "Five, four, three, two, one. You ready?"

"That wasn't seven minutes," Maddix heard Luke whisper. Maddix smiled as he said to Zennith, "Yup."

"So?" he asked. "What's your choice?"

Maddix closed his eyes, opened his palms, and fire erupted in them.

"How about you guess?"

CHAPTER 45
FLAMES AND WHISPERS

Why'd you give him time?" Sidero asked. "Why? They could teleport out of here at any moment!"

"Would you calm down, Sidero, it's fine," Zennith told him. "He can't teleport, and neither can his friends."

"How?"

"Remember?" Zennith said. "No one can teleport out of here."

"Ingenious," Sidero said. He looked over. "What are we going to do with them now that we've got them? And you know—when we lose them, it's hard to get them back."

"I know," Zennith said. "But I think I've stumped him for now; either way, he's doomed." Then he saw Parker look at him. Zennith nodded. He nodded back.

"Oh, looks like he's made his decision already," he said to Sidero.

"Quick," he said. "Say he's almost out of time."

"Alright," Zennith replied, looking at him questioningly. He turned to face the kids. "Five, four, three, two, one. You ready?"

Zennith heard Vincent whisper to Rader, "That wasn't seven minutes."

And he had to say, Parker looked pretty confident as he approached him. And after he asked, "So? What's your choice?" he knew why.

Maddix closed his eyes, and fire sparked into his hands. Zennith instinctively stepped back as Maddix said, "How about you guess?" His smile was so taunting, Zennith just wanted to step forward and unleash all he had on that little monster. He actually tried; as he took a step forward, Sidero grabbed his shoulder.

"Don't," he whispered in his ear. "I'll deal with him. You get Vincent and Rader."

Zennith nodded and slinked towards the two other kids while Sidero advanced.

"You know," he said (and was happy to see Parker wince as he spoke), "that fire there's dangerous."

"You don't think I know that?" Parker said. His tone was pretty strong to be standing in front of the greatest enchanter in the world—and, most feared—Zennith might add.

"Well, I have no doubt you were aware," Sidero said. "But sometimes people need a reminder. Now, what did you say your answer was?"

Maddix looked to his friends. He looked back. "Does this make it clear?" He launched a fireball at Sidero's head. The enchanter yawned as he deflected it easily. It crashed through the wall. Maddix looked at Sidero, the stun showing on Maddix's face.

Maddix tried again. "You think that's gonna stop me?" he said, the worry in his tone a little more easy to hear. Sidero knew his best bet was to make the worry only a little more visible...

Maddix tried to engulf Sidero in flames again, but the enchanter took the fire and re-directed it at Maddix's hands. Maddix tried to hold it, juggling the hungry flames. Finally, the flames were in his hands and they stayed there.

"Didn't anyone ever tell you not to play with fire?" Sidero asked, almost laughing. Maddix glared at him.

"You know what?" Maddix said. Sidero smiled. He could definitely hear the anxiety now. "You know what, why don't I blast you to pieces?"

Ugh, Sidero rolled his eyes, *even his comebacks are getting worse.*

Maddix raised his hand. Sidero didn't know what he was doing. Then, it hit him—literally.

There was a *BLAM!* and Sidero was blasted against the wall by the force of one of the kid's fireballs. *Oh,* he realized, *that kind of blasting.*

Maddix smiled at the villain's pain. "How'd you like that?" he said. Sidero stood up, rubbing his head. Then, he grinned as an idea hit him. He used his powers to lift Maddix up off the floor, hit the ceiling (hard), and crash against the wall.

"You know, I think I like *my* move better."

CHAPTER 46
ANGER AND FIRE

Maddix knew he was losing. He knew it as he hit the ceiling, then the wall. He knew Sidero could hear his worry—and that was a problem. And what had he whispered to Zennith to make him go for his friends? Now, he was face-to-face with Sidero, while Zennith hovered over his only hopes of help and advice.

"You know, I think I like *my* move better."

The words cut into him, making him want to lash out. Was he *asking* for the taste of fire? Did he *want* to crumble into ashes? Maddix stood up, a little unsteady on his feet, and launched his fire at Sidero once more—but more forcefully this time. Right then, he was just feeling *rage*—pure, undying rage that filled him from head to toe. And Sidero was going to pay for making it happen.

But, there was a problem: Sidero knew that, too.

"Getting angry never got anyone anywhere, you know," he said, his voice terrible and taunting.

"Now, I want you to *really* answer my question," Sidero said, walking towards him. "Not with actions, but with words. Of course, you know how to use words. At least, I hope you do."

"I do," Maddix said, thinking of something. "And I'm going to use them to escape." He ran to Nicole and Luke, whispering, "Teleport. Now."

"No," Nicole said hurriedly, "go outside and do it. Don't ask questions."

Too late—Zennith grabbed them, all three, and marched them to the door. He opened it.

"Outside, huh?" he said. "Good job, Rader. Super Hearing does come in handy, doesn't it?"

They struggled against Zennith's grip. Nicole glared at him.

"Let us go!" she yelled.

"Sorry, can't do that," Zennith said, smiling. He brought them closer to the door. Then, he shut it in their faces. Aside from wincing so hard he was sure Zennith could feel it, Maddix felt his face burning. They were caught. *Again.*

"You know," Zennith said, "we might consider something if Maddix here answers our questions."

"No way," Maddix shot back. "And it's 'Maddix' now? Not calling me Parker, are you? Well, you can't get me to answer your questions. I'm not stupid."

Zennith looked at Sidero.

"We were afraid you'd say that," Sidero said, coming over. "Actually, we were predicting it. So, we made a plan B." Maddix saw Zennith mouth, "We did?" And Sidero nodded quickly.

"What is it, then?" Luke asked. "Because nothing could get us to talk."

Sidero crouched down so that he was eye-to-eye with them.

"You think you're so *brave*, don't you?" he said softly. He put a finger to Luke's heart. "But deep down, you know that you're just three eleven-year-old children. Three. Eleven-year-old. Children."

"You can't change our minds about anything," Nicole said to them, sounding impressively confident with her face so pale.

"Yes," a familiar voice said behind them, "but we can change *yours*."

They turned to see the Magical Protection Force facing them. Maddix spotted Luke's dad, looking very disappointed.

CHAPTER 47
LISTEN

Zennith heard the whooshing noise, knowing Sidero heard it too. The Magical Protection Force was too quick for them. The head, Jack Lundren, used his powers to freeze the two villains. They couldn't teleport themselves, for they were stuck in the ice.

"Let's take these two bags of trash back to the OGM," he said gruffly. Two of the men carried the statues out the door. Lundren looked behind him; one his men was still there. "Vincent, you coming?"

Vincent, Zennith thought. *Who was he talking about? The kid?*

"Yes, but I'll be a minute," the last man said, his voice slightly muffled by the ice that surrounded Zennith's head. Zennith then realized that it was *Will* Vincent standing there, in Magical Protection Force uniform: black cloaks, with a red stripe, and black gloves. *He* was

242

part of the Magical Protection Force? Zennith wondered why he hadn't recognized him previously.

Zennith wanted to stay and watch what would happen. Did the kids come here unauthorized? If so, they'd be in trouble now. Zennith wished he had Super Hearing to hear their conversation as he was brought outside through the back door.

But, as he looked out the window, he saw Rader say something and Vincent's father hold them by the shoulder, steer them outside, and teleport away.

Lundren shrugged and said, "He'll be back soon," under his breath.

Zennith and Sidero were teleported with Lundren and one of his men to the OGM. The President, John Welsher, leapt up at the sight.

"Good gracious, Jack!" he cried. "What are you doing, bringing Zennith and Sidero into an office? Did people stare?"

"Sir, we caught them in that building in the east," Lundren said, not answering his question. "They were endangering three children: Maddix Parker, Nicole Rader, and Luke Vincent."

Welsher's eyes went wide. "Vincent, did you say? Will Vincent's son?"

"I believe so, sir," Lundren responded. "Where should we put them?"

"I'd say we destroy them at once," Welsher said, getting out of his chair.

(Zennith gulped.) "But where to do it? The giant hammer won't work; it'll just crush their ice, won't it?"

"I suppose so, sir," Lundren said. Of course, the good part for Zennith and Sidero was that he didn't think his answers through before he said them.

"Now, it's almost nightfall, let's sleep on it," Welsher suggested. "Keep them in the high-security room in the next hallway. If they try to escape—and I'm hoping and praying they won't, since I'm putting a guard there—we'll be monitoring on camera."

"One question, sir," Lundren said, turning to the ice statues. "Can they hear our conversation?"

"Hmm," Welsher went up to Zennith and poked the ice right in front of his face. Zennith tried his best not to move a muscle. Of course, Zennith couldn't move his muscles if he wanted to, but he tried not to make it look like he knew what was going on. This was surprisingly easy.

"You know, I don't think they can, Jack," Welsher said finally. "Put them in the room, I'll get Harold Patrick to watch them."

"Shall I fetch him, sir?" Lundren asked.

"No, no, I will," Welsher replied. "Now, get these two villains to the high-security room."

"Yes, sir."

In minutes, Zennith and Sidero were facing the stone wall of the high-security room. And Welsher wasn't wrong: cameras surveyed the scene, catching every sign of breath or movement. Zennith scanned the room, looking for any sign of traps or trip-ups. Harold Patrick was a strong-looking, stone-faced man who was much like Lundren. Pacing like a prison guard, he muttered to himself something Zennith didn't recognize.

Zennith tried to find the perfect moment to break out of the ice—it wouldn't be good to do it right in front of Welsher, not in front of Lundren.

So, it had to be when Patrick was distracted—

There.

He tried to look at Sidero, who was trying to look at him. They somehow knew what the other was thinking: *Now.*

After a split-second, the two beings used their powers to burn through the ice. Jumping out, Sidero used his powers to knock out Patrick and they destroyed the cameras. Studying the ground for any traps, they worked their way to the door. Getting into the hallway, they teleported and were gone.

CHAPTER 48
DISAPPOINTMENTS

L uke's father paced in front of them in his office, not even looking at their shame-stricken faces. Maddix stared at his feet, not daring to steal a glance. Luke fixed his stare on the opposite wall, unblinking. Nicole fiddled with her coat buttons, mouth firmly shut.

Finally, Mr. Vincent spoke.

"I am disappointed," he said. "*Very* disappointed."

"Dad," Luke began, "Dad, we—"

"I don't need explanations," his father put up a hand. "You disobeyed me by going out to seek Zennith and Sidero who, I repeat, are *highly dangerous*—"

"Mr. Vincent, you know we had a plan," Nicole said desperately.

Mr. Vincent looked to Maddix. "Maddix?"

Maddix sighed resentfully. "How much did you see?"

"We got here just in time to see *you getting your head cracked open!*" he exclaimed.

"What?" Maddix said, distracted. "That was a long time before you came in."

"Well," Luke's dad looked uncomfortable, "we had some—difficulties. Questions were asked by the head of the Force, Lundren. Jack Lundren. He's a know-it-all kind of person."

"So, after you answered his questions," Luke said. "Then you watched us be threatened by the two most feared enchanters in the world?"

"No," Mr. Vincent said. "We—er—we..."

"What?" Nicole prompted.

"Well... Jack's shoe was untied," Mr. Vincent finished.

Maddix, Luke, and Nicole shouted out in exasperation.

"But," Luke's dad said quickly, "but I kept urging him to do it fast, and as soon as he said he was done, we ran in there."

"I can't believe you," Luke said to his own father.

"No, I can't believe *you*," Mr. Vincent said, back to being serious. "I can't believe all of you. We went to security cameras, and found that you looked up the location of Zennith and Sidero on the computer. So, we went to the computer lab and went to the place you'd looked up." He looked at them sternly. "You not only disobeyed me by just *attempting* to find them, but by *teleporting* to their location, and *fighting* them."

"We weren't—fighting," Luke muttered.

"Oh, right," Mr. Vincent said, "you weren't *fighting*. You were *losing*."

Maddix looked at Nicole and Luke.

"You're right," Nicole said, "we were losing. And that was the problem. Thank you for saving us."

"You're welcome," Mr. Vincent replied, "but you apologizing doesn't change anything. Maddix, Luke, you're grounded for a month. Nicole—"

"Wait," Maddix interrupted, realizing something. "Mr. Vincent, my birthday's coming up. Is there a way I could *not* be grounded on my birthday?"

Mr. Vincent was silent for a moment. "You know what, fine," he said. "But after your birthday, Maddix, you have one more day."

"That's fine with me," Maddix said.

Mr. Vincent turned to Nicole. She gulped. "Nicole," he said, "due to recent events, I'm sorry, but—" he took a deep breath "—I have to expel you from Apollo Academy."

CHAPTER 49
SECRETS ARE MEANT TO BE KEPT

Zennith looked at Sidero in their secret hideout.

"What?" he asked.

"We've let them go again," Zennith said. "And Parker went into my mind."

"How do you know that?" Sidero asked.

"Because," Zennith responded, "when this all started—before we caught them—Parker was right next to me. Probably invisible. I heard Vincent has that power. So, Vincent must've ran out, because Parker turned visible again and ducked underneath the table. I heard a noise, but I was just too absorbed in my thoughts. Then, he whispered something in my ear."

"What was it?" Sidero asked eagerly.

"It was nothing important," Zennith said casually. But, as he threw those words out like they didn't matter, Parker's words echoed in his head: "Make sure you get the gist: Maddix Parker was here."

"Alright," Sidero said slowly. "So you think he went into your mind when he was invisible?"

"You know what, now that I think about it," Zennith said, "in order for him to go inside my mind, he would have to make eye contact with me, and he would have had to be right in my face. And I was looking right at the table. But *you* were facing the wall, so it would've been easier for him to make eye contact with you. What if—" He didn't finish his sentence.

Sidero's eyes went wide. "No," he whispered. "Do you think he went into *my* mind?"

Zennith nodded wordlessly. Sidero's eyes—if possible—went wider.

"What do you think he found out?" he asked. "There were all sorts of things, I bet. What did he see? Oh, no." His voice turned to a hoarse whisper.

"Zennith—*the prophecy*. He could've seen the prophecy!"

Zennith almost yelled out. "Ah!" he squeaked.

"I know!" Sidero exclaimed.

Zennith took a deep breath. "But—hey, what if there's a chance he *didn't* see the prophecy, huh? We don't have a confirmation he did."

"I know," Sidero said, "but we still need to be careful. Man, I wish I could go into his mind to find out if he saw it. But you can't have everything."

"I guess," Zennith said. After a moment, he said, "Let's go to the Room of Secrets. He could be there already, for all we know."

"Okay," Sidero agreed. "And if he isn't?"

"We wait," Zennith told him, "no one's ever there. It'll be fine."

"Alright," Sidero said.

"Wait, I have one more thing to tell you," Zennith said, as Sidero got ready to teleport. "Not that this is important or anything, but when Lundren was carrying us from the room, didn't you see Vincent, Rader, Parker, and Vincent's father teleport away?"

Sidero nodded.

"Well, before that, Vincent's father looked like he was being pretty stern with them. Like they were in trouble. You see where this is going?"

Sidero smiled as he nodded again. "Yes. So, you're thinking that, because they're in trouble, it'll hamper their plans of coming to fight us again. Very clever. They are such troublemakers. And you know what can happen when you're a troublemaker."

"You could end up in a tower," Zennith said knowingly.

"You just could," Sidero nodded.

"Come on," Zennith said, grinning, "let's go to the Room of Secrets."

Laughing, the two villains gripped each other's arms, swished their coats, and vanished.

CHAPTER 50
WHEN YOU NEVER LISTEN

N o!"
There was a ringing silence in the office.
Nicole? Expelled? Maddix's head was spinning.
What she did wrong wasn't school-related. He told this
to Mr. Vincent.

"I know, but she still did wrong," he said solemnly.

"But, Dad!" Luke exclaimed. "You can't expel her!
She's done so much to help!"

"But that has to stop," Mr. Vincent said. "You can't be
fighting those fights anymore. Just leave it up to the
adults, okay?"

"But—but we have to!" Luke said angrily. "Dad, you
don't understand—"

"No, *you* don't understand, Luke," Mr. Vincent said.
"You three have been in enough danger already. Some of
it you've been dragged into. The others—the others have
been by choice. And I am *very* disappointed."

252

Nicole inhaled. "I'm sorry," she said, her voice wavering. "I'll be in my room."

She walked out of the room, her face in her hands.

"Dad," Luke tried again, "did you see that? She's upset. And you said—"

"I'm sorry, boys," Mr. Vincent cut him off again.

Maddix and Luke went to their room and sat down on their beds, thinking.

"How are we going to get Nicole back to Apollo?" Luke asked.

"I don't know," Maddix said quietly. "What if we just—what if Nicole did some big project to show she shouldn't be expelled?"

"Good idea," Luke said. "But what?"

Maddix sat up. "So," he said, "what if something happened to your dad, and Nicole saves him? Maybe that could work?"

"Hmm," Luke said, thinking. "I think it will, but we have to make it look like it actually happened. And make sure it doesn't cause any real damage."

"Of course," Maddix said. "But, we're grounded, so we have to be *extra* careful. When's Nicole supposed to leave?"

"I heard my dad say tomorrow," Luke said.

"We have no time to waste, then," Maddix said, getting up.

That evening, Maddix and Luke caught up with Nicole in the halls. They told her about their plan.

"No," she said. "It's too dangerous. What if Luke's dad gets hurt?"

"He won't," Maddix reassured her. "And it's about you getting un-expelled."

"Well," Nicole struggled to find something wrong with it, but didn't succeed. "Well, I... guess it could work."

"Yes!" Luke and Maddix exclaimed. "Remember, be there when he—"

"Yes, I know," Nicole said, smiling. "This is kind of exciting, actually. I've never saved someone from a problem I created before!"

Soon, it was showtime. Maddix and Luke went into Mr. Vincent's office. He was surprised to see them. He got up.

"Dad," Luke said before he could speak, "we know we're supposed to be grounded, but we just wanted to say we're sorry."

From behind his back, Maddix called Luke on his cell phone. Luke's own phone rang as he was speaking (as planned) and Luke said, "Whoops, sorry, gotta take this. It'll be quick." (As planned) He took out his phone and said, "Hello? Hello?" Suddenly, there was a crash; Luke's phone was connected to a special bomb-like device in the walls where the wall could break at the push of a button. And that's just what happened.

Mr. Vincent fell backwards, into the broken wall.

"Oh no!" the boys yelled, acting surprised and trying to help him up.

Then, Nicole burst through the door. Just as a piece of the wall was about to crash down onto Mr. Vincent, she pushed him out of the way.

"Whoa, Nicole!" Maddix exclaimed. "What are you doing here?" Nicole rolled her eyes, though she was smiling.

"I was walking by," she said, "and I used my Super Hearing to know that you were in trouble."

"But, what you did," Mr. Vincent said hoarsely, "just now. How did you know that was about to hit me?"

Nicole shrugged. "Instinct, I guess."

"Thank you," he said, brushing himself off. He turned back to Maddix and Luke. "Well, I expect you should we be going back to your room now."

Maddix almost yelled, "*Seriously?*" But he caught himself. It wasn't over yet.

"Mr. Vincent, Nicole *saved your life*," he said.

"Saved?" Mr. Vincent said. "Maddix, I don't think she saved it."

Maddix and Luke looked at him, but his attention was on Nicole.

"Well, Nicole's there's a bus back..."

"Dad," Luke played his last and final card. "Nicole's been one of my best friends for not even a month yet.

And if she's expelled, I can't be in touch with her or anything—what if she's on the other side of the country?"

Nicole opened her mouth, probably to tell Luke's dad that she *wasn't* going to be on the other side of the country, but Maddix nudged her and she closed it.

"My point is," Luke continued, "Nicole's been a big help in everything. We couldn't have done anything without her."

"But she helped you do *wrong*, Luke," his father pointed out. "What she helped you do wasn't right. It was dangerous and inappropriate."

"But," Maddix said, grinning, "what she helped us do was get information for the OGM, and the Magical Protection Force. I'm sensing an Employee of the Month here. And, we *did* end up catching Zennith and Sidero, and that wouldn't have happened." He nudged Mr. Vincent, who thought about it. Maddix, Luke, and Nicole held their breath.

"Well," he said. He sighed. "I guess I can give Nicole one more chance."

The kids cheered.

"Just *don't*," Mr. Vincent said sternly, "don't go fighting Zennith and Sidero again. Or I *will* expel Nicole. No questions asked."

"Yes, sir," they said.

They skipped out the door.

"Maddix and Luke, you're still grounded!" he called after them.

CHAPTER 51
ENTRY

Zennith recalled that the Room of Secrets was as old as anyone could remember, the walls covered with writing in who knows what langauge. It was much like a cave, but the spaciousness gave it the title of a room. And it housed the *Book of Secrets*, so it earned the name the Room of Secrets. Anyone who wished to know any secret—any secret at all—would have to travel to the Room of Secrets and dare to open the *Book of Secrets*. The *Book of Secrets* has had the tendency to frighten people—and for good reason.

If an unworthy person opened the *Book of Secrets*, a strong wind would pick up and carry them all the way back to where they'd come from, and that person would not be able to go back to the Room of Secrets. It would just be impossible. Zennith thought it was kind of like karma: if that person had done good deeds in the past, the

Book of Secrets would let them see the secrets they wished to see. But if they had done bad things in the past, they would be whisked away.

Zennith and Sidero crossed the room, touching the worn pillars and feeling the rough walls.

"This really is an odd sort of place, isn't it?" Sidero said.

"Yes," Zennith said. "Are you going to touch the *Book of Secrets*?"

"No way," Sidero replied, "and I'm not going to open it, either."

"Yeah," Zennith agreed, "what happens to 'unworthy people' is pretty terrible."

"It'd feel pretty horrible to be that person," Sidero said, "and you can't come back to this room!"

Zennith rolled his eyes. "So, what should we do?"

"I told you, we wait," Sidero said, sitting on a bench. "If he read my thoughts, he will come here. And to pass time, we go over plans."

"For what we do when he comes?" Zennith asked.

"Or when *they* come," Sidero corrected him. "Parker could come with his friends."

"So, when he (or they) come, what do we do?" Zennith asked.

"Well," Sidero leaned in, "I thought we'd do something classic, like…"

He whispered something into Zennith's ear. He nodded.

"Interesting choice," he said, smiling. "I like it."

An hour passed, then two.

"What if they don't come for days?" Zennith asked.

"We'll wait that amount," Sidero responded.

"Weeks?"

"We wait."

"Months?"

"We wait."

"Years?"

"We wait."

"Never?"

Sidero looked at him. "Seriously?"

Zennith held his hands up. "What can I say? I don't like waiting."

CHAPTER 52
SLEEPWALKERS

Maddix and Luke spent the rest of the three weeks lying in their room, forced to do schoolwork (for the first time).

"I don't get why we have to do this," Luke complained. "I mean, we don't know any of this stuff!"

"Yeah, we do," Maddix said. "All this stuff is pretty obvious. Look—'In 1922, Albert Jacobs set out for a hike in the woods, though his friends urged him not to. What is the character trait of Albert Jacobs in this situation?'"

"Well, it's obvious, isn't it?" Luke said. "The character trait is 'headstrong.' He's a lone ranger."

Maddix laughed. "But don't you see?" he said. "*Your dad's shaming us through homework*, Luke."

Luke's eyes widened, then he started punching his book. "Stupid—dad—for—shaming—us—through—homework!"

Maddix lay on his back, laughing. In fact, he laughed so much, he fell off his bed. Luke joined him, laughing.

After a few minutes, they got up and resumed their homework.

Eight days later, as night fell, Maddix counted down the days until he turned twelve. As he checked off each day, he began to feel a sinking feeling in his stomach. Shouldn't he be fighting Zennith and Sidero? He shook his head. But, his eyes turned to the date today. November 29. His birthday was tomorrow. *Tomorrow.* He woke up Luke.

"What?" he croaked.

"It's time to work our magic," Maddix said. Luke nodded.

All they needed was Nicole.

That was the hard part.

They stepped into the hallway, whispering to be quiet. Maddix and Luke felt their way along, almost reaching Nicole's door when they heard footsteps. They froze.

Into their vision stepped Luke's dad.

"What are you boys doing?" he asked.

"Uh," Maddix fished around for something to say. "Sleepwalking." Luke stepped on his foot.

"Sleepwalking," Mr. Vincent repeated skeptically. "Okay."

"What are *you* doing?" Luke asked.

"Well, I'd hardly think that wasn't obvious," Mr. Vincent replied. "I'm patrolling. Bad things could happen at night."

Maddix and Luke nodded.

"Oh, hey," Maddix said, acting as if he'd just realized where he was. "Hey, look, Luke! We're in the hallway—and standing right here so let's go back to our room, bye!" Maddix turned Nicole's door handle and said, "Oh, wait, this isn't right…" He mouthed, "Invisible," to Luke, and Luke turned them invisible as they went inside.

CHAPTER 53
THE BATTLE OF THE ENCHANTERS

Sidero sat on the same bench, staring at the hard ground. It had been four weeks, why hadn't the kid come already? Everything he needed to know was right in front of him, but Sidero guessed Maddix thought it was just too dangerous. Sidero hated it when this happened, when people went soft because of others. So, because of the influence (of Vincent's father, he guessed), Sidero's enemy had gotten soft. Sidero was slightly disappointed. He not only wanted to destroy him, but he also wanted a purpose for a fight. Eleven years ago, there had been a huge fight: The Battle of the Enchanters, the biggest battle anyone could remember. Well, the most recent one, anyway.

The Battle of the Enchanters was the big fight between Sidero, Zennith, and their side, versus all of the other side. Everyone who spoke of the battle would remember the terror, the fear, the feeling of never being quite safe. Sidero had enjoyed seeing the panic in their eyes, the fright at the thought of facing him.

But it was all too good to be true.

Zennith and Sidero used all of their minions, all of their wits, powers, weapons, and plans to fight, but the other side got the best of them. On a dark day, as clouds blocked the sun and rain poured down, John Welsher used his powers to conjure a huge tidal wave, crashing over Sidero's army, and Sidero himself. Most of them got out alive, but they were too weak to fight. But Sidero didn't want to surrender.

The evening of the tidal wave, Sidero slipped, undetected, into a deserted courtyard and stood up against a wall, thinking. No one noticed him, as the whipping rain and hissing wind overwhelmed passersby, obscuring their sight.

Sidero started walking through the courtyard, thinking about what to do in the battle. He passed a couple of men chatting merrily about their sure victory against the evil. Sidero bared his teeth and kept walking.

He passed a leaning brick house on the other end of the gates. Sidero slipped through them and realized that the house was at the end of a nearby street. It caught his eye because, as said before, it was *leaning*. No other houses were leaning like this one. A straight, pearly white house was propped up next to it, looking important and highly sophisticated compared to its neighbor. Sidero, having nothing else to do, started walking towards the leaning house. He wrapped his cloak around himself, thinking it would be quite a shock for a local townsperson to walk right past the enemy, let alone *Sidero.* And his plan worked; no one looked twice at the warmth-clinging being next to them.

Sidero reached the house, and studied its windows. Someone once told him that you could judge a house by its windows, and if they looked how you liked your windows (whatever that meant), then you could assume the residents were fairly sane people.

But, as Sidero surveyed the windows, he noticed the people inside the building. There was a woman, with caramel-colored hair and piercing blue eyes, and a man, with darker brown hair that stuck up at the back and pretty much everywhere, and hazel eyes. Sidero seemed to recognize them. Where had he seen them before?

Then, it came back to him—earlier that week, Zennith had shown him a picture of a family of three. Zennith had said that he had been walking past their house and had sensed powerful magic coming from them.

"They must be destroyed," he had said.

Sidero looked back at the windows. Zennith had shown him a family of *three.* Where was the third person here? *Ah,* Sidero thought, *the third member of the family was a baby.* Yes, that was it. He remembered now. Sidero remembered; the baby looked almost identical to his father, but had the smile of his mother. Sidero hurried to Zennith and ordered him to zap the family's magical power at once. "Make it quick and clean," he told him. "But take the kid."

So, Zennith had gone. Nightfall had begun far before Zennith traveled to the house. The stars blinked as the servant walked silently along the streets of town, finally reaching the home of the family.

"Quick and clean," he muttered to himself. He opened his palms, and felt his power surging through him. He pointed at the windows, ready to strike.

And that's when it happened: Zennith's magic went terribly strong, and the windows crashed. The house was on the brink of falling down, and Zennith tried to fight the father. He remembered the house shaking, almost falling—

A deep rumble jerked Zennith from his thoughts.

The Room of Secrets shook.

Sidero stood up. So did Zennith.

"It's time," Sidero said.

CHAPTER 54
THE ROOM OF SECRETS

So, tell me *why* we're here again?"

They appeared on the brink of a river.

Teleportation didn't require the teleporters to know the specific location of their destination. All they had to do was think of the Room of Secrets, and they appeared there.

Nicole asked her question irritatedly, annoyed that Maddix and Luke had woken her up. Stars twinkled and the clouds settled in. Luke looked up.

"Nicole, we told you," Maddix said, "we're here to fight Zennith and Sidero, and to defeat them once and for all."

"Why can't you *not* be such a hero?" Nicole said, smiling slightly.

"So, what's your plan, Maddix?" Luke asked, still looking at the sky. "'Cause we better hurry. I think a storm's coming in."

"I don't think so," Nicole said, looking at the clouds, "it might just be cloudy."

"Well, either way, Luke's right," Maddix said to them. "We have to get a move on. They're probably just waiting for us in there."

"Alright, so what's your plan?" Nicole asked.

"So, we go in," Maddix said, "and we act like we're all afraid, to make it seem like they have the advantage."

"Good, I'm liking this," Luke said.

"Then," Maddix continued, "when they start sneering like they do, like they have control—"

"We blast them to smithereens at the last second," Nicole finished, excited.

"Exactly," Maddix said. He looked across a stream and saw the awaiting cave. "So, are you ready?"

"Always have been," Luke said.

"And always will be," Nicole said.

They found a nearby log and used all of their strength just to push the heavy log over the water. After they made their makeshift bridge, they stepped gingerly across it.

Then, they reached the cave. Maddix and Luke climbed around the side to the top of the entrance, and Maddix launched fireballs at the roof of the cave. Bits of it came crashing down.

"Nicole, look out!" Luke warned.

Nicole dodged the falling rocks, and Maddix and Luke climbed back down.

"Come on," Nicole said, "let's get in before the rocks cover the entrance!"

So, the kids ran in, their hands over their heads, yelling, "Avalanche! Run!" Maddix used his fireballs again, and the falling rocks burst apart, leaving the entrance open.

Maddix noticed Zennith and Sidero sitting in the middle of the room, and said, not looking at them, "Wow, that was close. We could've died." He breathed fake gasps, hoping he wasn't overdoing it.

"I know," Nicole said, wheezing. "I've never run so fast."

"Uh, guys?" Luke said shakily, pointing to Zennith and Sidero. "Th-they're *right there.*"

"Ah!" Nicole squeaked. She ran behind Maddix. "Do you have a plan?" she whispered loudly in his ear.

"No," Maddix whispered back, just loud enough for Zennith and Sidero to hear. "I just thought I would think of something as we came in here."

"Why didn't you think of something, then?" Luke whispered.

"Well, I was a little preoccupied with almost dying from an avalanche, thank you!" Maddix exclaimed. To his delight, he saw Zennith and Sidero exchange eager looks.

"Excuse me," Sidero said, walking towards them, "I had the impression that this was *our* room?"

Maddix almost decided to sprint to the far wall in fear, but he hadn't acted like that before, so he thought it would be pretty suspicious if he acted like that now.

"L-listen," he stuttered slightly, "we c-come in p-peace."

"You know, I don't think you do," Zennith said. His voice got high-pitched when he said, "You know, I."

"*Maddix*," Nicole said through gritted teeth, "*hit them with fire or something. Do something!*"

"I can't," Maddix said through gritted teeth, "it's a little—"

"Whoa!" Luke exclaimed, pointing at the two villains. "Maddix, Sidero's got ice! He's got ice!"

Maddix tried to step on Luke's foot without Zennith and Sidero seeing. They were overselling it.

Zennith repeated Luke in a mocking tone. "*Maddix, Sidero's got ice! He's got ice!*"

Sidero laughed. "Yeah, I've got ice," he said, tossing it the air and catching it. "And I might just—whoops." The ice slipped from his hand and hit Nicole squarely in the face. She stepped back, and almost lost her act. Her face went burning red, and she was about to unleash something pretty serious on Sidero (and say some not-very-nice words to him as well), but instead she stepped back with a scared look on her face. Thinking it was very unnatural to be hit in the face with an iceball and not be angry, she glared at the two villains.

"You know, I could hit the daylights outta you!" she exclaimed. She fake lunged; Maddix and Luke grabbed her by the arms and held her back.

"Really?" Sidero said. "I don't think your friends want you to."

"Wait for a plan, Nicole," Maddix whispered loudly in her ear.

"Yes, Rader," Zennith said, "listen to the guy in charge."

Nicole went red. So did Maddix. Luke took charge.

"Listen, you two," he said to Sidero and Zennith, "if you just came here to talk, we'll just be leaving." He turned to Maddix and Nicole. "Come on, guys."

They started to leave, but Zennith used his powers to pull them back to Sidero.

"Look," he said, "you three have something we want. And all we came here to do was get it. Now, if you would just give it to us, we'll be on our way."

"And what about w-what we want?" Maddix asked, fake gulping. "W-what's in it for us?"

"You get to walk out of here, no damage done," Sidero told him, "but if things go wrong, you'll still walk out of here—but, mark my words: *there will be damage.*"

"So much damage they might not be able to walk out of here," Zennith whispered happily to Sidero. Maddix, Luke, and Nicole heard. They didn't like it.

"So, we're making another deal with you," Sidero said. "All you have to do is give us what we want, and we'll let you go free."

"But," Zennith said, "if you don't, there will be a fight."

"A big one," Sidero added.

"Huge," Zennith agreed.

And deadly, Maddix thought. His mind whirred. What were they going to do? Maddix wished he could send Luke and Nicole a telepathic message: *Stick to the plan.* Luckily, they were already thinking along the same lines.

"Um," Nicole said. She looked around. A shadow of a smile flickered on her face. "Can we have time to think about it first?"

Zennith looked at Sidero, laughing. "No, you can't. So, come on. Remember, Parker," he looked at Maddix, "the clock is ticking."

Maddix grinned. He nodded to Luke and Nicole. It was time to show the villains how the three of them *really* fought.

"I know that," he said, his voice way different now. "But I think the clock is the least of our worries."

CHAPTER 55
ACTORS

It was obvious Parker and his friends were acting. It was just too obvious. Their expressions, their exclamations, their actions, everything was all acting. So it was no surprise to Zennith when Maddix started speaking in a totally different voice.

Maddix's eyes flared with anger and power as he said, "But I think the clock is the least of our worries." And, about that sentence—he was wrong. The clock *was* the biggest of their worries.

The kid went straight up to Zennith and Sidero— well, almost. He was going to, but while walking, Sidero blasted him to the ground. Maddix skidded and slid all the way to the other wall.

"Adorable," he said, grinning.

"What are you calling adorable?" Luke yelled to him.

"Your efforts," Sidero turned to him, the look in his eyes saying, "Oh, you want some, too?" He added icily, "your efforts are just adorable. *Amateurs.*"

"Who're you calling amateurs?" Nicole shouted. Zennith was surprised. She usually didn't speak, and when she did, it was a scared squeak.

"You," Sidero said, digging the knife a little deeper. "I'm calling you three children amateurs. You *inexperienced, unprofessional* little amateurs."

That got them good.

Maddix got up and looked straight into Zennith's eyes. He made the DWAH face, and—

CRASH!

He was sent soaring back to the wall, and his eyes were glazed before they closed.

"You see what I mean?" Sidero said to Zennith. "Complete amateurs." They laughed.

Luke advanced towards the two villains, but Zennith flicked his arm lazily and both Rader and Vincent were tied up in ropes.

"Maddix!" Rader yelled. "Maddix, we need you!"

From the other side of the room, Maddix's eyes opened.

CHAPTER 56
MIND GAMES

Maddix sat up. He rubbed his head. *Why* did the floor have to be so hard? Then, all his thoughts came back to him: Zennith, Sidero—they were *right there*! And Nicole and Luke were tied up! *Ah, geez,* Maddix thought, annoyed, *guess it's just me and the bad guys.* Unfortunately, that was a situation he hated to be in.

Nicole's words echoed in his head. They needed him. There was no turning back now.

He faced the two villains. Maddix knew he couldn't walk toward them again; his head already had enough damage done to it. If they wanted to fight with him, they'd have to walk to him themselves.

"Hey!" He cupped his hands around his mouth, shouting. "Hey, what's the holdup? Are you too *scared* to come near me? What, are you gonna come closer or no?"

Zennith smirked. "Alright, if you want to be so strong now—you'll get what you want."

They walked a few steps closer. Then a few more. Then a few more. Maddix rolled his eyes. *Are you kidding me?* Then, he smiled. They were already slow, so why not slow them down just a *little* more?

He launched fireballs at the two villains, so they had to step back in order not to get scorched.

Maddix snorted with laughter as Zennith grabbed Sidero's arm. They kept backing away. Fireball after fireball. Step after step. Luke and Nicole noticed what he was doing and Nicole grinned broadly. Luke sniggered. Zennith saw.

"What are you—?" he then looked at Maddix, who hid his hand behind his back quickly. But he wasn't quick enough. Zennith lunged forward but Sidero held him back.

"I'm gonna crush that kid so hard he'll wish he'd never been born!" he said through gritted teeth.

Maddix stepped back. Now he was scared.

What would Zennith do?

Keep it together, the voice in his head was back. *Don't let him get to you—Sidero too. They're just trying to make you mad enough to do something stupid. Just keep calm and don't give in.*

Right, Maddix told it. Thanks.

Any time, kid, it said, *now focus before that Zennith guy kills you!*

Maddix shook his head. The voice in his head was right. Maddix blasted Zennith to the other wall with his fireballs.

"You're not touching me!" Maddix said. Sidero advanced. Maddix raised his hand to use his fire, but, in seconds, Sidero was holding him by the collar of his shirt.

"*Don't,*" he said, "or you'll be very sorry."

Maddix kicked him in the stomach. Sidero let go, gasping for air.

"Hey!"

Maddix was tempted to bolt out of the room, but then he realized this was his one and only chance to destroy Zennith and Sidero.

He reared back, and ran straight at Zennith. Fire erupted in his hands and he burned Zennith so badly the villain couldn't even stand up. The man lay on the floor, gasping. A few seconds passed, and Maddix fired another fireball. Zennith dodged, but that seemed to take up all of his energy. Zennith lay still.

Now—to Sidero.

Maddix didn't know how to destroy someone who he was sure wasn't a mortal. Could he use fire again? Maddix looked to Nicole and Luke for help. Nicole nodded to Luke, who nodded back. She mouthed, "Combine the fire." Maddix wondered what she was saying for a second—then it hit him. And good timing, too: Sidero had recovered and faced him.

"So," Sidero said, "what are you going to do now? Sure, my servant's down, but you've still got me to defeat. And, I've got your friends tied up, so they're not much help. And *whispering* doesn't help, does it?"

Oh, it does, Maddix thought with satisfaction, *you have no idea how much it does.*

"Now," Sidero continued, "I hope you have a plan, because I'm going to destroy you just like Zennith destroyed your ex-Firecatcher father."

That *does* it.

Maddix ran again to Sidero, summoning as much fire as he could in the span of five seconds. Sidero raised his hand to blast him away, but Maddix was too fast. He launched a fireball at the wall to the right, and it ricocheted forward. A split-second later, Maddix fired a fireball at the left wall, and it flew towards Sidero. He flung two more fireballs at the front and back walls, and they all joined together, forming a huge shooting star. Maddix then thought of another thing: he reached in his pocket, and used the Electro Pencil to shoot electric beams at the shooting star, making it considerably more violent as it hurtled toward Sidero. It looked like it was full of fireworks, fizzing angrily and red-hot. It hit Sidero squarely in the chest, and Maddix's shooting star was so forceful, Sidero went through the rock wall.

Suddenly, the walls shook, and rocks started to fall as the cave broke apart. Maddix ran over to his friends and carefully used fire to cut the ropes. He knew Nicole disapproved of him using fire so close to them, of course, but no one speaks about that kind of thing when they're about to be crushed by rocks.

"Come on!" Maddix yelled over the sound of the rocks.

"*What?*" Nicole and Luke shouted.

"Over here!" Maddix shrieked. Luke and Nicole followed him, running, to the podium where the *Book of Secrets* sat.

Suddenly, Maddix had an idea. Praying it would work, he focused on Zennith's actions months ago, when he had first met him. A Sound Field. Finally, he got it: a blue force field surrounded them. The crumbling rocks collapsed around them, but they didn't touch them.

When the crashing stopped, Nicole spoke.

"W—what happened?"

"Yeah, what's that?" Luke asked shakily.

"A Sound Field," Maddix replied. "Zennith used it when he was talking with me the first night we saw him. Do you remember, we ran into Nicole's room?"

"Yeah," Luke said, like he'd rather forget about that part.

"Well," Maddix said, looking at the *Book of Secrets*, "what should we do with this?"

"It's obvious," Nicole said. She looked at Maddix, and her tone grew softer. "Find out what really happened to your parents, Maddix."

Maddix opened the *Book of Secrets*. He held his breath.

CHAPTER 57
IN THE RUBBLE

Zennith opened his eyes. He didn't know how he survived the room collapsing, but he did. Or, at least he thought he did. Zennith looked around. Yup, he was still alive. He sat up. His head ached terribly. His eyes moved around the scene. It was miraculous how all the little rocks had landed either on him or beside him.

And, in the middle of it all, a Sound Field around them, were Parker, Vincent, and Rader.

He almost got up, but then he noticed: *Sidero wasn't there.* Where was he? Suddenly, a terrible thought struck Zennith—what if Sidero was *dead? No,* he thought quickly, *Sidero can't be killed just by rocks. He's Sidero, for goodness sake!* That calmed him down a bit. His master was still alive.

But where *was* he?

He didn't notice the Sidero-shaped hole in the wall next to him.

Then, the Sound Field disappeared. Zennith noticed that *Parker had the Book of Secrets!*

Zennith smiled. Didn't he know that whoever was an unworthy person and opened the *Book of Secrets* was sent back to where they came from and could never come back? Surely, Parker was one of those people.

Apparently not.

Mouth hanging open, heart in his mouth, Zennith watched as Parker opened the *Book of Secrets*. He noticed that the kid was holding his breath. So he knew what would happen if he wasn't a worthy person.

Zennith still couldn't believe that Parker had actually opened the *Book of Secrets* and, by now probably, was even reading from it! He couldn't comprehend it!

Suddenly, his vision was clouded. *Oh,* he thought, remembering his huge burn, *I forgot about that.* His head felt heavy. His closed his eyes and his head thudded against the ground.

CHAPTER 58
THE SECRETS

Nothing. No wind, no going back to Apollo—*nothing*.

"Come on, Maddix," Luke said, "look there!" He pointed to the Table of Contents.

"How are we going to find his parents in a gazillion other names?" Nicole asked.

Just as Maddix said, "I don't know," he spotted golden letters shining in the middle of the page. Though the writing was miniscule, Maddix could read the names: *Christopher and Abigail Parker.*

"Hey, look, it's them!" Maddix exclaimed, pointing. "Page... 204."

"Go on, then!" Luke said eagerly.

Maddix leafed through the pages until he found page two hundred four. There it was. Maddix read it aloud:

"On a cold winter's evening, during the War of Enchanters, a leaning brick house was surveyed by the one and

only Sidero. In the windows he saw a family of three: a mother, a father, and a baby son."

"That's you, Maddix!" Luke said.

"We *know*, Luke," Nicole told him sharply. Her expression softened. "Read on, Maddix."

Maddix continued, *"The father, Christopher Parker, was the last Firecatcher to be known, descended from Raven Parker. Christopher had learned a great deal about the evil enchanters.*

Abigail was much the same (though she learned a little more about the evil forces than Christopher did).

So, you can imagine, the two adults were ready when Sidero sent his servant, Zennith, to destroy them. But the only problem was: what about their son?

Their son was one years old, named Maddix. He didn't have the slightest inkling what magic or evil was, let alone how dangerous Sidero could be.

That night, Zennith approached the house. He was a more anxious man at this time, and when Sidero gave him orders he hastened to fulfill them—but sometimes, they didn't work out too well.

Zennith struck down the door. It blew off its hinges, sending wood spraying everywhere. The walls shook with the force. Christopher, upstairs, heard a crashing noise and came running down. Abigail, in the kitchen, hurried to the front door—or, rather, what was left of it. Abigail screamed at the sight of the evil servant, and Christopher leapt right into a fight.

But Zennith didn't want to fight. Quick and clean, Sidero had ordered. So, quick and clean it would be. Zennith tried to take Christopher's powers as a Firecatcher before he could make his first move. He did, actually, but it didn't work out how he'd planned. His magic was much too strong, and Christopher was blasted to the wall, which crumbled on top of him. Zennith turned to Abigail as the house came crashing down. He used his powers again, a little more controlled this time, but his powers were still too strong, and his move sent the whole house crumbling.

No one knows what happened to Christopher and Abigail; they assume they were killed by the house collapsing on them.

But the story doesn't end there. In the ruins of the house, a strangled cry met Zennith's ears. He searched through the rubble and retrieved the little boy, Maddix. And, with that, he teleported to meet his master again."

Maddix closed the book with a snap. Most of it, he knew or could assume. But *Zennith* had killed his parents? And by *mistake*? *Well,* he thought, *you know from the story that he was going to destroy them anyway.* But, he thought, it felt pretty good to be related to fighters. His father didn't go down without a battle. His mother was right by his side.

After a few moments, Maddix had processed. It was alright now. And he'd gotten revenge. He'd destroyed Sidero, hadn't he? He couldn't be sure. But at least he'd slowed him down from evil for a long time.

"Hey, hey, Maddix," Luke said, looking at his watch. "Look what time it is."

"What?" Maddix and Nicole crowded around Luke.

"Five... four... three..."

Oh. Right. His *birthday*. But what would happen when it struck midnight?

"… two… one."

Suddenly, there was a blinding, golden light. Without warning, Maddix felt himself spinning, and spinning, and spinning…

It was over.

Just like that, it was all over.

Maddix opened his eyes. He was on the floor again. Oh *why* was he on the floor whenever he opened his eyes?

Luke and Nicole were looking at him weirdly. It was almost as if they were in awe.

"What?" Maddix asked, getting up. "What are you staring at?"

Nicole pointed a shaking finger at him.

Maddix looked down.

He gasped.

He knew at once that he was different. For one, his clothes were. He'd seen the uniform of the good enchanters, the Magical Protection Force, that helped with fights. Fights like the War of Enchanters. They wore black cloaks striped with red, and black gloves.

"You…" Luke said. "You look like one of those warrior enchanters! That's so cool!"

"I know, right?" Maddix said.

Nicole rolled her eyes. Leave it to the boys.

"This is serious, guys," she said. "Maddix, you told us about a prophecy, right? In Sidero's mind?"

"Yep," Maddix said, still admiring his gloves. "What about it—oh." He realized.

And as years pass, and the boy turns twelve, evil's last standing will never be held.

"You mean, I completed the prophecy?"

Nicole nodded. Luke said, "Whoa." Maddix grinned.

Months whirred by, and soon it was June 1. The students went back home on June 3.

Maddix, Luke, and Nicole spent their last couple days sitting outside and looking at the grass flow in the wind. They were particularly happy today, though; Mr. Vincent had just told them that Dagner had been found in the janitor's closet and was arrested.

When Mr. Vincent left, Maddix asked, "Why do you think he was arrested?"

"Um," Luke said, smiling, "I might've told my dad he pushed you into a mirror. And, for once, he believed me. Well, after I told him about the Thunderbirds. And the manticores. And the Thunderbirds again."

They laughed. It was fun to have no evil to worry about and live normal lives. But, if any evil came, Maddix always had his powers and his enchanter's uniform ready.

All too soon, June 3 came. Nicole boarded a Flying Bus and said good-bye to Luke and Maddix.

"I'll see you next year!" She called as the bus pulled away.

"Wish she could come here during the Summer," Luke said.

"You know, I wonder if we could go to her place," Maddix said thoughtfully.

"Yeah, since we have a wonderful background with her parents," Luke said.

The two boys laughed. And right then, Maddix knew that this Summer was going to be the best one of his life.

ACKNOWLEDGEMENTS

First, I'd like to thank my dad for helping me with putting this project together, and being my wonderful editor. I still can't believe how much time he put into this, and I am incredibly thankful for him.

Second, I give props to my sister, for writing the foreword for this book, and putting in the time to write it.

I would like to thank all the inspirational people in my life who have helped me spark ideas and put them into words—I cannot explain how different this would be without my inspirations.

And lastly, I would like to thank my whole family together, for supporting me through the process of writing.

ABOUT THE AUTHOR

Algebra Carter lives in Palatine, Illinois, with her family. She has written the novel *Liam Stone and Private Tower,* and co-wrote the short story *Experiment 42.* Alongside writing, she loves reading, playing volleyball, and spending time with her family. She recently entered the sixth grade.

Follow @AlgebraCarter on Twitter
Visit her blog at AlgebraCarter.com
Buy her books on Amazon

Made in the USA
Lexington, KY
12 September 2017